Three years ago, Cohen Brandwein was a teenage media-darling, a popular author and internet celebrity. But ever since he came out as trans, public opinion has been less than golden, and these days he wants nothing more than to escape the big city and find somewhere quiet to work on his next book.

When he inherits an old house in the Irish countryside, Cohen sees it as a perfect opportunity to get away from it all. What he doesn't count on is becoming embroiled in a paranormal murder mystery, and falling for the primary suspect, a handsome but mysterious self-proclaimed witch, whose reality makes Cohen's fantasy books seem like child's play...

TO SUMMON
NIGHTMARES

J.K. Pendragon

A NineStar Press Publication

www.ninestarpress.com

To Summon Nightmares

Printed in the USA

ISBN: 978-1-64890-372-4

First Edition, August, 2021

Also available in eBook, ISBN: 978-1-64890-371-7

CONTENT WARNING:
This book contains sexually explicit content, which may only be suitable for mature readers. Depictions of death, gore, self-harm, dysphoria, misgendering, depression, domestic abuse, guns, incarceration, kidnapping/abduction, murder, torture, and trauma.

Chapter One

NOVEMBER, 2007

Jacky had crawled into Niall's bed in the night. Niall thought about waking him and telling him to go back to the thin foam mattress on the floor, in case one of his parents walked by and saw them together through the crack of the door. But the floor was wood, and the house was old, and winter was setting in. Sleeping on the floor was cold, but Niall knew that wasn't why Jacky had crawled into the bed next to him.

He stirred, and Jacky's thin fingers grasped at his nightshirt, his legs wrapping tightly around Niall, and he muttered something in a soft and frightened voice. His hair, black and shiny with grease, fell limp in front of his sunken eyes. He was so beautiful, Niall thought, knowing he was the only one who saw it. He wrapped his arms tightly around Jacky, wishing he could protect him and keep him safe always. But Jacky couldn't spend every night at Niall's. He would have to go home tonight. Home to *him*.

"Niall!" His mother's voice from down the hall spooked them both awake; Jacky's eyes flew open in a panic. He jumped away from Niall and hurriedly scuttled under the blankets on the floor as the sound of footsteps grew closer and Niall's mother pushed the door open.

"Morning, boys!" she announced, and Niall and Jacky pretended to wake up, rubbing their eyes and gazing blearily at her. "Oh heavens, it's freezing in here; you've left the window open all night!"

Well, that explained the chill. She stepped over Jacky, who shrank away from her, to shut the sticky window tight. "Time to get up or you'll be late for school. No more sleepovers if you're going to be exhausted the next morning. What time did you boys go to bed last night?" She cocked her head, hands planted on her hips.

Niall and Jacky looked at each other guiltily. "Not that late, Mam," said Niall. "I dunno. We didn't look at the clock."

"Well, get dressed." She tutted. "Honestly, you boys don't appreciate me. You think all mothers allow sleepovers on school nights?"

"No, Mam." Niall managed a smile through bleary squinted eyes. "You're the best, Mam."

"Well, you've got that right. All right, up, breakfast's almost ready."

She left, closing the door behind her.

Jacky sighed and lay back on the pillow. "Why can't I just live here with you, Niall?"

Niall bit his lip. "Well, y'know maybe if you told her, like, what's going on with your dad—"

"She won't listen," said Jacky crossly. "They never listen. I told you. And me dad told me if I made a fuss again he'd hit me harder." He flinched, his eyes going dark. "He said he'd kill me last time. I *told* you, Niall."

"I know, but I bet Mam *would* let you stay here."

"She wouldn't, Niall. Anyway, I don't wanna talk about it. We're doing it tonight, aren't we?"

"Yeah, I said tonight, didn't I?"

"You sound like you don't want to."

"Of course I want to!" Niall jumped down onto the floor and grabbed Jacky, pulling him into a tight hug. "Hey, we've been planning it for weeks. I'm not gonna back out now."

"Bet y'are though," said Jacky, sniffling.

"I'm not." Niall took Jacky by the arms and looked him firmly in the eyes. "I'm not just gonna abandon you, Jacky. Whatever it takes, I'm gonna take care of you. I love you."

"I know." Jacky sniffled again, rubbing his eyes. "I just can't go back there again. I can't keep lettin' him—"

"You won't." It hurt deep in Niall's heart to see Jacky cry. He couldn't stand it. He pulled Jacky to him and kissed him hard, hoping it would stop the tears and take away some of the fear. "Listen, I got it all planned out. Everything's ready. I'm gonna be there tonight at midnight sharp, okay? We're gonna do it."

"You promise it'll make him stop? You promise it'll work?"

"I promise, Jacky. I know what I'm doing. I've been studying this stuff for years; you know that. Magic works. I've tried it. You saw the stuff I can do."

"It's just little stuff." Jacky crossed his arms.

"Yeah," said Niall, feeling slightly offended. "That's just 'cause I haven't tried anything big yet. Look, if you don't believe me, I'll prove you wrong tonight. Right?"

"Yeah." Jacky sighed and turned away to look for his clothes. "I hope it works, Niall. I dunno what I'll do if it doesn't."

"It'll work," said Niall. "Don't worry."

It was impossible to concentrate at school. Niall's mind was running through the ritual, remembering all the incantations. He'd be reading them out loud from a book tonight, but he had memorised them all anyway. He doodled the summoning circle in the margins of his notebooks, over and over again, so he'd have it perfect. It had to be perfect.

Jacky wasn't in any of his classes this year. He had been in years past, but last year Jacky's grades had slipped, and he'd been placed in learning support. Niall had tried to help him. Tried to make him learn. But his attempts had only been met with acidic responses and eventual tantrums from Jacky. He was smart, but no one could make him learn. So Niall had decided to leave it alone. He would learn when he was ready. *And this might just change everything.*

Jacky met him at lunch, in their usual spot outside the gymnasium. It was a corner that no one ever came near, so they were in relative privacy. He leaned his head on Niall's shoulder and sighed. Niall drew him close, savouring the moment of aloneness. "How's class?"

"Just stupid," sniffed Jacky. "I can't really think. I'm so excited."

"Me too. I've been practising."

"I got on the computer a little." Jacky stiffened a little and leaned away from Niall to grab his bag. "I printed out some stuff."

"What?" Niall leaned forward.

"Well, I thought—" Jacky pulled some papers out of the bag, printed articles. "I thought we might make a last-minute change."

Niall bit his lip. "I don't know, Jacky. It's kind of a delicate thing."

"Who's the one you want to summon? *Densel*?"

"Denusel," corrected Niall. "Well, he seems best; I mean, I looked him up in a bunch of different demonology books, right? He's supposed to be really good at persuasion and mind control, so I figured he'd be a good fit. Plus, it said he had an even temperament."

"It's just..." Jacky frowned, chewing on his nails. "He's not supposed to be very powerful, is he?"

"He'll be enough, Jacky; it's all relative. This is a really simple request, like a small transaction. The more powerful demons are much more dangerous, and they do much bigger stuff."

"Yeah, but if you do it all right, it'll be fine. It won't be able to hurt us."

"It's— Sure, but we don't need to—"

"Because I looked it up, and I found this." Jacky shoved the article at Niall. It looked old like it had been photocopied from a book, but not one that Niall had ever seen before.

"*Khireneth*," he read aloud. "*Notably powerful demon, recordings include*— No, this is no good. It doesn't say anything about his power level or what he does."

"It does down here, see?" Jacky pointed. "Look, it says he calls himself 'Champion of the Oppressed.'"

"Sure, but that doesn't mean anything; demons are all liars. They're bad and dangerous unless you know how to contain them."

"I know. You told me, but you *do*, right?" Jacky swallowed. "I want to make sure it works. I want to be sure."

"I am sure."

"Niall, I want to do this one."

"No."

"Please. Please, Niall." Jacky blinked and a tear rolled down his face. "It has to work. There's no other way. My dad—"

Niall clenched his jaw. He hated that man. And he hated even more that there was nothing he could do. Jacky wouldn't let him tell the teachers, or the police or anything. Not since he'd come to school with a black eye once in fourth grade, and the teachers had sent a social worker to their house. Niall didn't know what Jacky's father had done to him as punishment, but he never talked about it. And when Niall even suggested telling someone about it, Jacky went white as a sheet.

Niall hated feeling helpless. That was probably why he had taken up magic. It gave him a feeling like he had some control over his life; that he could help. And he could help. If this summoning went well, why couldn't they summon a more powerful demon? The transaction would be the same. And it would be a for-sure thing.

"Okay," he said. "Okay, Jacky, we'll do it."

★

He nearly tripped several times on the long walk from his house to Jacky's. He'd left a little after eleven at night when he was sure his parents had gone to bed already. They slept early because his father worked a morning shift at the nearby prison, and were often asleep before Niall. The climb out his bedroom window had gone surprisingly smoothly, but he'd neglected to bring a torch, which was proving to be a fatal mistake.

"Ow!" He stumbled over another rock and almost fell, the bag of supplies heavy on his back and throwing off his balance. The dirt road was uneven and peppered on the sides with brambles and rocks and the occasional fence. It was a peaceful walk, other than the rocks, no vehicles to drive by at this time of night and wonder why a sixteen-year-old was walking along the road in the middle of the night.

He stared up at the night sky, the gloom of clouds breaking occasionally to reveal the deep-blue sky and twinkling stars. He was never out this late, and the view was glorious. "Ouch! Christ!" He lost his footing again and forced himself to stare at the dim path in front of him, away from the endless sky.

He could see the dark shape of trees and Jacky's house up ahead and pulled out his mobile to check the time. Close to midnight. He stopped for a moment to let his eyes adjust back to the dark and then hurried on.

Jacky was waiting for him on the back porch, like they'd planned. "You're smoking again," said Niall, eyeing the glowing ember in Jacky's fingertips. "Why d'you have to do that, Jacks?"

"I'm nervous." Jacky dropped the finished cigarette and ground it under his foot. "'Sides, he likes to punish me for stealing them whether I do or not. Might as well get the benefit out of it, right?"

"Make yourself sick," sighed Niall, and Jacky nodded at the heavy pack on Niall's back.

"It's all in there?"

Niall nodded. Adrenaline was coursing through his veins. His first summoning. Excitement and terror sizzled in him like sparks. He felt almost overwhelmed with the anticipation. "Your dad's asleep?"

"Drunk himself into a stupor." Jacky lifted his shirt a little to show Niall the newly forming bruises on his pale ribs. Niall longed to kiss the bruises better, but he knew Jacky didn't like them touched. Besides, this wasn't the time for sex. "He's upstairs," said Jacky. "Like I thought. Come on; cellar's this way."

The rusty lock rattled a little as Jacky unlocked it, and Niall looked around nervously.

"It's fine," Jacky reassured him. "He's not waking up tonight."

The door creaked open, and Niall had to run to catch it from slamming down. Skinny limbs trembling, he and Jacky pushed it back into place, ducking under as they did so, letting it close on top of them, leaving them in utter darkness. They sat on the dusty cement stairs for a little while, breathing heavily until their eyes adjusted to the darkness and Niall could make out the stairs leading downwards to the cellar. He'd been down here before, always during the day though. They had played down here as children, and then later used it as a hideout for secret make-out sessions.

"This way," said Jacky, rushing ahead. He grasped the yellowed cord hanging from the ceiling and pulled, flooding the cellar with dim light from the bare, dusty bulb. Old boxes and skeletal wooden shelves cast long black shadows into the dark corners, and they seemed to move. Niall told himself it was just his eyes playing tricks on him, but he was anxious to get this over with now. He pulled the heavy pack from his shoulders and set it on the ground, crouching to remove the contents.

He retrieved the old book with the summoning ritual (to blame for most of the heaviness), and another binder with instructions he'd printed online. Then there were the candles, a sturdy lighter, two boxes of white chalk, and a knife to cut them open. Finally he pulled out a tape measure and enlisted Jacky's help to create the summoning circle.

"Does it have to take this long?" asked Jacky, after about twenty minutes of measuring and planning. "You haven't even started yet."

"It'll be faster once I've done the prep," said Niall. "It has to be perfect, Jacky; it's very important."

"I know." Jacky wandered over to look at the contents of the book in the dim light. "I'm just nervous."

"Me too." Niall straightened and went to the bag, then pulled out the first box of chalk. He dug the knife into the thick cardboard of the corner and sliced it off, creating a small spout for the chalk to pour through. "Okay, now to business."

He drew the circle, walking around the circumference and pouring the chalk over the lines he had traced in the dirt, the box in one steady hand and a paper with the image of the circle in the other. It had to match perfectly. Once he had drawn the main lines, he moved onto the details, opening the second box of chalk along the way. He was glad he'd thought to buy two.

When the time came to print the demon's name around the circle, he hesitated. He could just do Denusel; Jacky wouldn't know until it was too late. But no, he couldn't deceive Jacky like that. He'd decided on Khireneth, and Khireneth it was going to be. He printed the name in neat block letters, one on each side of the circle.

Jacky was bored at this point, sitting on a crate and watching Niall with his chin in his hands. "A year off each of our lives," he said. "You're sure that'll be a good enough sacrifice?"

"That's what it says in the book," said Niall distractedly.

"But what if we're meant to die tomorrow? What would happen then?"

"Then he'd probably refuse the offer. But it wouldn't matter that much anyway, since we'd just be dying tomorrow."

"How would he know, though? Can demons see the future?"

Niall stood to survey the circle once more. He almost had it right, but he had to be sure before placing each line. The chalk wasn't forgiving. "Some of them, I think. I don't know; they all have different powers."

"Wouldn't it be nice to have magical powers, Niall? I mean, not like the little spells you do, but real magic. Could solve all your problems that way."

"Mm, I imagine it'd drive you a bit evil, honestly." Niall stepped forward, carefully placing his feet in the space between the chalk and then leaning forward to draw another precise line. "I mean, if you think about it, demons are probably evil *because* they have so much power, not just because they're a naturally evil race. Power corrupts you, right?"

"Not always, I don't think. Some people with great power do really great things. Like superheroes."

"Superheroes aren't real, Jacks. Okay, I think I'm done."

Jacky rolled his eyes. "Yeah, you say you're done, but you're gonna look it over another ten zillion times first; I've seen you do this stuff."

"Yeah, you're right." Niall stared at the circle on the floor, and then back at the paper, and back at the floor again, until the image was burnt into his mind. He went and picked up the book, and stared from the image on the page, and then to the floor, and then to the page again. Impatience gnawed at him, but he ignored it. This was very, very important.

At last, he pronounced himself properly done, and Jacky jumped up to survey it. "It looks awesome."

"Now I just have to place the candles."

Jacky sighed. "That'll take another age, won't it?"

When it was at last complete, Niall looked at his mobile, surprised to see that it was nearly one thirty in the morning. He didn't feel tired at all, his body practically vibrating with anticipation. "All right, let's do it. Jacky, come stand over here. I need you to read with me. Did you memorise the lines like I told you?"

"I did actually."

"All right, stand here, Jacky." Niall took Jacky's hands in his and kissed him. "I love you."

Jacky's lip was trembling. "I love you too, Niall, and I'm sorry about this."

Niall shook his head and reached down to grab the book. "Don't be sorry," he said. "I'm doing this for you because I want to. It'll make everything better."

Jacky nodded in agreement.

"All right." Niall looked down at the summoning ritual on the page. "Now, here and here's where you say Khireneth. You *must* pronounce it properly. *Khireneth.*"

"Khireneth," repeated Jacky. "Got it. Here and here."

"Good," said Niall. "All right, on the count of three." He took a deep breath. "One. Two. Three."

They began to read. Perhaps it was only because they were concentrating on the book, but it seemed that the light dimmed and the candles flickered, despite the lack of wind. At first their reading was clumsy and awkward, but soon they began to pick up speed, their voices merging together effortlessly. They spoke faster and faster, until Niall was sure the words were speaking themselves, forcing themselves out of his mouth. There was no going back now.

A darkness was forming in the centre of the circle, a darkness that was not simply a shadow or an absence of light, but a darkness that banished light in the way light normally did darkness. The candles underneath it seemed to shimmer and dim, until they were all but non-existent, like blind spots in the corner of Niall's vision.

His tongue slipped over the word *Khireneth*, like the slicing of a sharp knife, and then again, and it felt as if a thick powder were working its way up from his lungs to fill his mouth. Like chalk. He resisted the urge to cough and kept going. Jacky's voice was strong beside him, but he choked a little too. As they reached the bottom of the page and the end of the incantation, it became almost impossible to talk, to breathe, to think. His mouth was filling with chalk, his vision with darkness. He no longer saw the words; he was reciting from memory, or from desperation. At last they came to the end and he spat out the last three words. "Khireneth, Khireneth, Khireneth."

The last sound felt like the air escaping an unstopped bottle, and all sound hissed from the room. The candles blew out; the darkness expanded to envelop all. And then the darkness receded. The candles flickered back to light, and the sound came back into the room.

In the middle of the circle stood a man.

Niall wasn't surprised. He hadn't been expecting a hell beast or horns or anything of the sort. He knew that demons liked to appear as humans. To humans, at least.

He heard Jacky cough beside him and quickly turned to help him. Jacky hunched over, coughing until his voice became hoarse, while Niall held him. At last he straightened, his eyes watering. Niall felt the need to cough, too, but he forced it down.

The man was watching them patiently. It was difficult to look at him somehow, as if disrespectful. But that was probably just his demon's influence. They were in control here.

"Hello," said the demon in a bland English accent. His voice was surprisingly normal. He sounded like a BBC newscaster, or a politician. "My name is Khireneth. What's yours? And where, might I ask, am I?"

"Don't tell him your name," said Niall to Jacky, who nodded.

The demon looked pleased. "Good decision," he said. "But I deduce by your accent that we are—" He looked around. "—somewhere in Ireland? Go on, say something else."

Niall gritted his teeth. "We're not gonna tell you where we are."

"Somewhere near Cork, I'd say, but not quite that urban." He looked around again. "The countryside?"

"You don't know that," said Jacky, speaking up, although his voice wavered. "We could be anywhere, and just come from Ireland."

"Ah, but you both have the same accent."

"We might be brothers," said Niall desperately.

"Oh, don't try that," said the demon. "You're obviously lovers."

Niall felt his face blanch. No one had guessed. No one. They'd kept it such a good secret. And now this man had figured it out within a few minutes. "Never mind that; we have a proposition for you."

"Oh, and here I thought you'd just invited me round for tea."

"The—" Jacky swallowed. "The books say you call yourself Champion of the Oppressed."

The demon turned his head to look at Jacky, and Niall suddenly realised why the demon's appearance was so off-putting. His eyes were a bright, sunflower yellow. He raised his eyebrows at Jacky. "And you fancy yourself oppressed, do you? Yes, you do. I can see it in your eyes. Well, I would love to help. In exchange for something else, of course."

"Right, yes," cut in Niall, feeling the conversation was slipping out of his control in an uncomfortable way. "We'd like to offer you a year off each of our lives, in exchange for your help."

The demon turned those yellow eyes on Niall. "And what on earth would I do with that?" he asked.

Niall stuttered. "Th-the book said—"

"Yes, I'm not quite sure how I feel about your book, boy."

"My father," said Jacky. "I want him gone."

"Yes?" said the demon, staring down Niall. "And is that your offer or your request?"

"W-what?" gasped Niall.

"Are you—" The demon paused, his yellow eyes darting between the two of them. "—offering me the boy's father, in exchange for something from me?"

"No!" said Niall, but at the same time, Jacky cut in.

"What could you give us?" he asked. "In exchange for my father?"

"Are you mad?" cried Niall, but the demon had already turned to Jacky.

"In return for the body and soul of a wretched man?" He smiled. "So very, very much."

"No, J—" Niall gritted his teeth. He had to get Jacky's attention. "You can't!"

"Could you give me magic?" asked Jacky. "Like, powerful magic, like you have?"

"But of course," said the demon. "If that is what you want."

"It's not what we want!" said Niall. His heart was racing, his fists clenched. Jacky was about to make another one of his stupid decisions, and he had to stop him. "Our bodies aren't designed for that kind of power; it'd kill us!" He didn't know if that was true or not, but he needed Jacky to listen to him.

"On the contrary," said the demon. "It would take some practice, but the right person, I think, could wield such power fabulously."

Jacky had a strange look in his eye. Niall grabbed him, forced him to look at him. He wanted desperately to say his name, had to stop himself. "You can't do this. Your father—"

"My father deserves whatever he gets," said Jacky, his voice calm but full of vitriol at the same time, his eyes wide and terrible. "Niall, we have to do this!"

Niall could hardly comprehend what Jacky was suggesting. How could someone he loved even be *considering...*

Jacky turned back to the demon. "All right, I'll do it."

"No!" said Niall.

"Niall." Jacky turned to him. "Shut up."

The demon was standing, his arms crossed, and a finger on his chin. "And who do I listen to?"

"Me!" said Niall. "I'm in charge here!"

"Really?" said the demon. "It doesn't seem that way."

"I accept your terms," said Jacky. "My father is sleeping in the bedroom on the top floor. You can have him in exchange for the power you spoke of. For me and Niall."

"I don't want it!" Niall gripped Jacky's arm, tried to pull him away from the demon, but Jacky retaliated, knocking him away with a swift blow. Niall fell backwards, too surprised to react.

"You'll thank me for it, later," said Jacky. He turned to the demon. "Do it."

The demon smiled and nodded at the knife discarded on the ground. Niall lunged for it, but Jacky got there first. "Blood," said the demon, and Jacky put the knife to his palm, and sliced it open. Niall was crying, begging Jacky over and over, but Jacky wielded the knife at him when he tried to approach. He reached out for Jacky once more, and Jacky sliced at him, drawing blood from his arm.

Jacky grabbed him with his cut hand, smearing their blood together. The demon was at the edge of the circle, farther than he should have been able to go, holding a palm up to Jacky. Blood dripped from a sharp cut there, glinting in the candlelight.

"No, Jacky!" cried Niall, but Jacky reached up and pressed his palm to the demon's.

"Say the words," ordered the demon. "Release me, and it shall be done."

Jacky said the words, quickly and effortlessly. He must have memorised them too. Or the demon had given them to him. His voice was liquid and gravel, and then Niall felt chalk in his throat again, and he began to choke. Darkness swooped over them; the candles extinguished. Niall choked again, harder, desperately drawing in a breath. And then it felt as if, along with the air, the darkness entered, pushing deep into him.

Then the pain began, and there was nothing else.

★

His body felt stiff when he awoke, but for a moment all he could feel was relief that the pain from last night was gone. It had gone on for hours, ripping through his body, pain like he'd never felt before. He'd broken his leg once, when he was eleven, and the pain he'd felt then was the closest he had ever come to this. But he hadn't wanted to die then, hadn't wanted it to all be over, just so the pain would stop. Last night he'd wished for death, wished he had never been born. But still the pain had continued, white hot and burning and tearing him apart from the inside. He'd been unable to see, unable to feel anything but the pain, and to hear his own screams mixed with Jacky's for hours and hours. When sleep had finally come, he'd clung to it desperately, letting it drag him down into oblivion.

Now it was all over. The pain was gone, blissful relief in its stead. There was a light shining, insistent, behind his eyelids, and he was stiff from lying on the cellar floor. He opened his eyes and coughed at the dust he lay in, looking around for Jacky. Light streamed down from the open cellar door, sparkling on the dust motes. The remains of the summoning lay strewn about him, melted candles and lines of chalk, scuffed and smudged by his writhing in the night. His bag lay open, its contents scattered, and he noticed, his mind hazy, that his books were missing.

His eyes were stinging from the dust. He rubbed them and rolled over onto his back to stare at the ceiling. The light bulb was still burning, dim compared to the bright morning sunlight. Where was Jacky? He must have left, because the cellar door was open, and they'd closed it last night. Why hadn't he woken Niall?

The sound of his mobile ringing startled him. The ringtone was familiar, oddly so, as if it belonged to something from a past life. It was coming from his bag, where he'd stashed his phone last night. He leaned towards the bag, several metres away from him, and suddenly the phone was in his hand.

What? No, that wasn't right; it had been in his bag, across the room. He stared down at the phone in his hand, the small screen lit up with an incoming call from his parents. Shit, his parents. He flipped the phone open and held it to his ear.

"Hullo?"

"Niall, thank god! Where the devil are you?" His father's voice was loud and angry with a note of panic.

Niall groaned, rubbing his eyes again. "I'm fine, Dad. I'm at Jacky's. I—I spent the night."

He heard his father relay the information to his mother, and then her gasp of relief. "What kind of game are you trying to play, son? You have to tell us where you're going, you know that!"

"I know, Dad, but it was important." Niall screwed his eyes shut, trying to think. There was something he was forgetting. Something important.

"Oh? And what was so important?"

"I have to—" Niall shook his head. "I have to find Jacky, Dad. I think he's done something horrible."

"What? All right, Niall, stay there; your mother and I are going to come get you."

"I...all right." He had begun to shake, as if his shoulders could no longer support his weight. His hands were trembling, and his stomach felt sick. Jacky. What had Jacky done? "See you soon." He snapped the phone shut, swallowing hard. "J-Jacky?" He took a deep breath. "Jacky!"

No answer. Slowly, he stood, shoving his phone into his pocket and struggling to find his footing. He stumbled up the stairs, flinching in the bright light. "Jacky!" The door to the house was open, banging against its hinges in the cold breeze that had picked up overnight. Niall stepped inside, his footsteps echoing on the grimy linoleum floor. There was a reason Niall never spent the night here; the place was a dump. There were beer bottles everywhere, perched precariously on the edges of counters and littering the floor, and the buzz of flies sounded from the dish-filled sink.

He called Jacky's name again, wanting very badly to leave. He wandered over to the sink to look at the flies, swarming over an old ground beef package. One buzzed near his face, and he swatted at it distractedly. He felt his hand make contact with the insect's body, and then a flash of sizzling heat. The fly's body dropped to the floor, and smoke began to rise from it. Niall stared at it.

That sickness was back in his stomach again. He backed away from the sink, lifting a hand to stare at his palm. It looked perfectly normal. What had happened? What had he done?

"Jacky!" he called again, hearing his voice croak with panic. He turned to run—he didn't know where—and nearly ran into Jacky. His face was close to Niall's, his eyes bright, and his mouth forming a wide smile, and Niall felt the strange urge to back away.

"Niall!" said Jacky, his hands clenching around Niall's arms. "Niall, he's gone! I've looked everywhere; he's not here!"

Niall tugged away, trying to break free of Jacky's iron grip. "Who's not here?"

Jacky's grin expanded. "Who do you think? My dad. He's gone! The demon did it!"

"Gone?" Sickness. Sickness in the pit of Niall's stomach, spreading through him. He was going to retch. "Gone where, Jacky?"

Jacky shook his head, his eyes still wide and wild. "What does it matter? He's gone! Niall? What's wrong?" Niall felt himself collapsing and Jacky reached forward. Suddenly there was a chair right under Niall, where he could have sworn there wasn't one before. "Did you see that, Niall? Did you see what I did?"

"Jacky, you've got to calm down." Niall forced himself to breathe. Forced himself to think. For Jacky. "Something...something bad has happened to us. Something dangerous."

"It's not dangerous," said Jacky. "I can—" He turned suddenly to look out the open door. "Who's that?"

"My parents," said Niall. "Jacky, we should tell them what happened. We need to go to the hospital or something." *You need to go to the police.* But what would he tell the police? That they'd summoned a demon? That Jacky had—

"Niall!" His mother's voice was coming from the drive, and he could hear the car doors slamming. "Niall, are you here?"

Jacky was tugging on Niall's sleeve. "Come on, let's go talk to them."

Niall forced himself to stand, to walk to the door with Jacky. His parents were coming. Everything would be okay. Everything would get sorted out.

"Mrs. Daly!" called Jacky, stepping into the cold wind. "Mr. Daly, hello!"

"Jacky, what's going on?" Niall's mother squinted as Niall emerged after Jacky. "Niall, thank god!" She pulled Niall into a tight, comforting embrace, but Niall pulled away quickly. He shouldn't touch her. It wasn't safe. Not until... He swallowed.

"Mam," he said, his voice cracking.

"What's going on, Niall?" she said, smoothing his hair from his face. "Why did you run away last night?"

"I was gonna come back," he said. "I didn't mean to worry you."

Niall's father was peering around Niall into the house. "Is your father here, Jacky?"

"My father?" said Jacky. "My father doesn't live here."

Niall swung his head around to stare at Jacky. Was he going insane? Niall's parents *knew* that Jacky lived here with his father, ever since he was a child. "Jacky, what?"

But Niall's father was looking at Jacky curiously. "Oh, of course, you're right. I'm sorry."

"Nothing bad's happening," continued Jacky. "Niall just spent the night."

"No," said Niall. "No, something bad *is* happening." He could feel something at the back of his throat. Like a lump of energy, like something he could spit out along with his words. But he didn't want to.

Jacky was doing it, though. He could hear that energy in Jacky's voice as he spoke, explaining that Niall had spent the night like they'd planned, and they were just heading out to school now. His parents nodded at him, their eyes strangely glazed.

"Mam, Da, stop. We need to go to the police." The lump at the back of his throat again. He could *make* them believe him, if he wanted to. But he didn't. The thought made him sick. "Jacky, what are you doing?"

"Hush, Niall, it's fine," said Jacky. He was grinning at Niall's parents. "So we'll see you tonight," he said.

His parents blinked rapidly, as if the glaze was clearing from their eyes, and then Niall's mother pulled him close for another hug. "See you tonight," she said. "Love you."

"Mam!" he shouted, but she was already turning away, heading back to the car.

Jacky turned to Niall, a look of triumph on his face as the car drove away. "Did you *see* that?" he squealed.

"No, Jacky. *Jacky.*" Niall let that energy pervade his words now, although it didn't seem to have much of an effect on Jacky besides making him smile widely at Niall.

"Ah, look, you can do it too! Brilliant!"

"It's not, Jacky. You—it's not brilliant; it's dangerous! What if you hurt them?"

"I didn't hurt them. I just persuaded them. It's magic! Like I asked for! Like you do!"

"It's not what I do!" said Niall, his voice becoming louder as he spoke. "That's black magic, Jacky. It's dangerous! It's not safe; you could hurt them! You could seriously damage them. Do you understand? My parents!" He choked. He began to cry. The warmth of his mother's hug was slipping away.

Jacky looked concerned for a moment. "I'm sorry, Niall. I didn't think."

"You're right; you didn't!" said Niall, forcing back tears. "You've done something awful, Jacky, and we need to figure it out. I don't know how, but somehow we've got to get rid of these...these *powers* before we hurt someone!"

Jacky shook his head vehemently. "I don't want to get rid of them though. I'm finally free."

Niall's heart dropped into his stomach like a rock, sending ripples of disgust and despair through him. "Jacky, your father is *dead.* You killed him!"

"I didn't," said Jacky, reaching for Niall, who tore his hands away. "Niall, the demon did it, not me!"

"You..." Niall's legs gave out again, and he sat down heavily on the porch. He pressed his face into his hands.

What was he going to do? There was something wrong with Jacky. Something he hadn't realised before, although he should have. The person standing next to him, the person he *loved*, wasn't who he thought he'd been at all. Was this what had been lurking under the surface all along, just waiting to come out?

"We've got to get to school," said Jacky matter-of-factly.

Niall looked up at him, incredulous. "School?"

"Yeah. Why, what do you wanna do?" Jacky's face lit up. "Niall, we could do *anything*."

Anything. He could do anything at all. But what *should* he do? That was the question. "Let's just go to school. We'll figure something out tonight."

They walked to the bus stop in silence, Niall's mind racing, but when the bus came and they boarded it like every other day, he could almost convince himself everything had been a horrible dream. They sat in their normal seat near the back and huddled together while the other kids talked loudly and noisily about their plans for the weekend. It was like normal. Maybe everything could just keep being normal.

Except how could everything go back to how it was when... No, he couldn't think about it. Not yet. Just follow the routine. Say goodbye to Jacky, open his locker, collect his books, and slump to class.

He sat in the same chair, in the same room, with the same teacher's voice wafting over him. Yet everything was different. He could feel things about the room that he hadn't been able to before. He knew things. Things he couldn't possibly know. The teacher's first name was Mitchell, and he was going through a divorce with his wife. The girl next to him thought she might be pregnant and was going to kill her boyfriend. The boy in front of him, the one who always teased Jacky and called him queer, was thinking about fucking men, picturing it vividly in his head.

No! It was too much pressing into him; he was going to go mad. He stood abruptly, and the entire class turned to look at him. "Niall?" asked the teacher, the one with the cheating wife and the secret sock fetish who wished his mother hadn't left him as a child—*no, stop it!* "Is something wrong?"

"It's nothing," said Niall, his mouth dry. "I just have to go to the toilet."

There was a knock on the door, and the teacher turned from the strange look he was giving Niall to go answer it. Two men stood there, one with pale skin and short ginger hair, the other bald with dark-brown skin. They wore plain black suits, and their eyes were frighteningly similar, cold and narrow.

"Hello," said the Black man, his eyes glancing around the room. His accent was smooth and English, and Niall was reminded of Khireneth, the memory accompanied by a burst of nausea. "We're here to collect Niall Daly. It's a family matter."

"Oh," said the teacher. Niall was still getting information from him, spurts of childhood memories, colours, flavours. But from the two suited men, he got absolutely nothing. Wasn't that strange? "Of course. Niall?"

Niall stood frozen for a moment. Family matter. Had something happened to his family? Something Jacky had done to them? His stomach lurched. "Coming," he said, quickly reaching back to grab his bag and rushing to the front of the room. "Are they okay?"

"Your parents are fine," said the ginger man in an Irish accent indiscernible from Niall's own. "This is about you."

"I don't understand."

"You will shortly. This way."

They led Niall out of the school, and Niall thought for a moment that he should check out at the office. But if this was really an emergency...

The two men led him to a black van parked in the lot and pulled the door open. Niall only glanced in for a moment before he began to scream for help. Jacky lay on the floor of the van, his eyes closed and his body still. Niall couldn't tell if he was alive or dead. His scream was cut off by the Black man, who clasped a hand over his mouth. Niall tried to scream, but he could barely breathe. The man's hand smelled like sweat and metal.

"Get him in." He nodded to the Irish man, glancing around nervously. Niall tried to struggle, but they were much too strong. He tried to remember what he had done to the fly, the flash of heat, the burning.

"Ouch!" said the Irish man. A few strange words escaped his mouth, and Niall felt the fire being extinguished as if doused. "You don't want to do that," hissed the man. "Your friend tried to struggle." He jerked his head at Jacky, and Niall's eyes widened, panic setting in. The men managed to get a proper grip on him and tossed him into the van, the door sliding closed behind him.

Niall screamed, shoving himself at the door, lashing against it with everything he had, his fists, and his new raw magic that he was so terrified of. It *hurt*, touching the metal walls with both skin and magic, shocking him and burning him, until he was nearly sick and unconscious, crying on the floor.

"What's going on?" he whimpered, crawling towards Jacky. He reached for his face, touching it, trying to wake him. "Jacky, wake up, please!"

"He won't wake up for several hours," said a tinny voice from somewhere above him. It was the Irish man. "No point in trying."

"Who are you?" Niall said, his voice shaking. "Where are you taking us?"

"Somewhere safe," replied the voice. "We belong to an organisation called the Guild. It's in charge of regulation and control of magical practices."

"Magical practices," whispered Niall. "But we didn't *do* anything."

"Not yet," said the voice with a tinge of amusement. "But you've caused quite a stir. Your power levels registered on all the charts, out of nowhere too—much too dangerous to leave without Guild intervention. I suspect they'll want to detain and study you. It won't be too bad. A few weeks at most if you cooperate." There was a pause. "It's for your own good, you know. Power like that is dangerous. Could cause serious problems if left unchecked."

"Yes," said Niall, feeling his heartbeat subside a little. "I suppose that's true."

The voice didn't respond, so he crawled to the middle of the metal floor and lay down next to Jacky, taking his hand and squeezing it. "You hear that, Jacky? They're taking us somewhere safe. Everything's going to be fine."

Everything was going to be fine. Everything was going to be just fine.

Chapter Two

OCTOBER, 2012

"You were crying in your sleep again."

Kathleen opened her eyes, giving up on the desperate desire to fall back asleep that always accompanied the loud buzzing of the alarm. Warren was lying on his side next to her, his head resting on his arm, just looking at her. He reached a hand out to smooth a few stray blonde hairs out of her eyes.

"I'm all right," she said. "Just bad dreams."

"I know," he said, his thick black eyebrows knitting in concern. He was so handsome, even with the worry lines that had formed around his dark eyes as of late. He reached out his arm, and she let him pull her into his embrace for a few moments, sighing in the momentary contentment.

"I don't want to go today," she said, her voice so quiet she could barely hear herself.

She felt him sigh, knew he was suppressing an old argument. "You don't have to."

"Yes, I do. You know that."

"I wish you could at least tell me what you're doing."

"I'd rather you didn't know, honestly." He would leave her if he knew. Surely he would. She was always surprised he didn't leave her anyway. She pulled him closer, willing him to stay.

"I'll make the coffee," he said with a quick peck to the side of her head. "Rest a little longer."

"Yeah." But she didn't. Once he was gone she lay between the cold sheets and tried not to think about the day, to no avail. Finally she got up and pulled on a soft white robe, exiting into the sparse, modern kitchen. "Did you check on her?" she asked Warren, nodding at the closed door down the hall.

"Sleeping," he said. "You wanna say goodbye to her before you leave? She has another treatment today, so she'll probably want to see you." He held out the coffee cup and Kathleen took it gratefully.

"I'll pop in and say goodbye before I leave," she agreed. "What time is it?"

"The appointment? Two o'clock. You won't be able to make it."

"No." She sighed. "You'd think they'd at least let me go with her."

"I don't like any of it." Warren leaned against the counter, sipping his coffee and staring angrily off into the distance. "If they have the technology for the treatment, why don't they make it available to the public?"

"If they did, it'd cost a fortune, and I'd have to work for them anyway to pay for it."

"You could work somewhere else."

Kathleen shook her head. The coffee tasted like ash. "Doesn't work that way. I'm contracted and specialised."

"You're miserable."

"We all make sacrifices for our children," she said quietly. Warren knew that. He'd given up a promising law career to care for Mina so that Kathleen could work full time for the company and continue to receive "benefits." Warren was right; they *should* make the treatment available to the public. But that wasn't the Guild's style. Kathleen was valuable, her sick daughter's treatment collateral, and that was the way it was.

She couldn't bring herself to wake Mina fully from her slumber when she went in to say goodbye. The treatments were painful, and she needed all her strength. She smoothed the dark hair off her daughter's face and kissed her forehead, worrying at the pallor of her skin. She never seemed to stay healthy for long. Kathleen often wondered why the Guild didn't possess magicians capable of healing her completely. But she knew the answer, if she thought about it. They did, of course.

Mina shifted a little and murmured Kathleen's name—she had never picked up *Mummy* and *Daddy*. Mature from a young age, just as Kathleen had been. Although for Mina it was out of necessity, not precociousness. Kathleen continued to smooth the girl's hair out of her face, whispering that she had to go to work now, and that Warren would be taking her for her treatment later today. "Go back to sleep now," she whispered, watching Mina's eyelids flutter into rest. "I love you."

"Love you too," whispered Mina, and then she was out again.

Kathleen sighed, willing herself to stand from where she had been crouched next to Mina's bed. She had already changed into a sharp grey business suit and pulled her hair back into a tight bun. She longed for the days before the Guild, when she'd worn her hair free, braided with bones and crystals. Silly nostalgia that didn't bear thinking about, but some days she couldn't help it. She wondered what Baba Mina would think of her now.

She was glad the old lady was dead. She could hardly bear the shame as it was.

"Have you got a lunch?" Warren asked her as she slipped into her pumps at the door, and she shook her head. "You've really got to eat."

"You're nagging," she said.

"I'm worried."

"Yes." She reached for her bag, slinging it over her shoulder and straightening her jacket. "You've made that abundantly clear."

He stepped across the kitchen to stand in front of her, bringing his hands up to her face. "Have a good day," he said, pressing his lips to her forehead. She wanted to laugh, but was afraid it would come out as a sob. She wished she could tell him. She wished she could confess.

★

She had barely swiped her card to enter the facility before she was accosted by workers, swarming around her and informing her of an "ongoing incident with Subject J6."

"Is he trying to escape again?" she asked, not in the mood for the sort of technical terminology encouraged by the Guild.

"N-no, not exactly," stammered one of the secretaries, shoving his glasses further up his sweaty, beak-like nose. "We can't seem to discern a motivation; he's just gone haywire!"

"Any damage to the facility?" She reached for one of the clipboards shoved at her and surveyed it momentarily.

"No," said a young woman, far too young, with pretty brown eyes and hair. A novice Sorceress put on grunt work in the hopes of achieving a high position. Kathleen always had to force down the desire to tell her to run, to get away while she still could. But it was too late anyway. "He's contained, but we thought you might be able to calm him."

Kathleen sighed, stepping into observatory room J6 with another quick swipe of her card. The glass viewing window was dimmed to block out the painfully bright light from within the holding room. If she squinted, she could see a dark figure moving around inside, erratic and blurred. "How did he manage to break free of the restraints, then?" she said, sighing again.

Another young Sorcerer stood with his hands on the magical charge panel, feeding energy into the magical blockers of the walls. "It was our fault, ma'am," he said, his teeth gritted. "We didn't switch shifts quick enough, and he waited for the break. Must have been building up reserves all night."

"He's secure now, though?" she confirmed, peering at the dim figure of J6, still darting around the room in a frenzy. The sound transmitters had been turned off, but she knew if they weren't she would be able to hear the crashes as he threw himself repeatedly into the magically reinforced walls.

"Yes, ma'am," said the Second Hand who had risen from his seat when Kathleen entered. "He'll exhaust himself eventually, and we'll be able to restrain him then. Unless you think you can calm him now."

She tapped her foot, staring disapprovingly at the glass. "No," she said. "He's just having a tantrum. Let him wear it out. I'll work with J7 for the morning. You're all right on shift there, then?" she said, eyeing the Sorcerer, who was sweating slightly.

"Fine," he said. "Normal wear, really. I'm just out of practice."

"You've been on J7, haven't you?" she asked.

The man nodded. "He's pretty slack."

"In some ways, yes." She spared one more frown at the figure beyond the glass before leaving, assigning two more Sorcerers to the room, just in case. Her pumps clacked against the metal floor as she made her way down the hall to the J7 observation room. She couldn't help but feel relieved that she wouldn't have to deal with J6 until later in the day, even though she liked to get him out of the way. Oh well, nothing to be done for it.

She swiped her card once more and stepped into the J7 observation room The Sorcerer on duty, who had been slumped with only one hand on the charge panel, straightened guiltily and nodded at her, while the Second Hand barely swivelled in his chair to glance at her.

"Anything new?" she asked, setting her bag down on the counter and straightening her jacket.

The Second Hand shook his head, barely glancing at her. "He's been up for a few hours. Usual routine, don't you usually do J6 first?"

She shrugged. "Bit of an issue with 6. Will you let him know I'm coming in?"

"Sure," said the Hand as Kathleen left through the side door into the tertiary chamber. "I'll tell him to put a shirt on."

She sighed, crossing her arms as she waited for the magical seals to travel from one door to the other. The Sorcerer was taking his time about it. At last, the light above the door glowed green, and she pulled the door open and stepped into the suite.

The sparse white decor was cold and clinical, but it was a sight better than the metal restraints J6 lived with. J7 had earned these luxuries through cooperation and submission. For every experiment done without incident, every mind search and memory probe without resistance, he gained favours. Little things like clothes, books, furniture, and limited internet access. Kathleen liked positive reinforcement. She wished she had the chance to use them on J6, but he only ever forced her into negative reinforcement.

There was a rustling from the bedroom, and a moment later J7 emerged. He was barefoot but wearing jeans and a T-shirt, ones he had requested, and he was newly shaved and washed. He liked to take care of his appearance, keeping his hair short and working out every day on the exercise machines provided. Kathleen knew it made him feel like he was holding on to his humanity.

"Hello, Kathleen," he said, his Irish accent as pronounced as ever. Sometimes she wished she had never given him her name. It felt more real this way. More damning. "You're early."

"Hello, Niall," she said. "Why don't we have a seat?"

"Are you going to torture me again today?" he said with a small smile as he sat on the couch across from her. "Or will you be getting into my head and making me think I've escaped when I haven't again? That was fun."

"I think we're a little past that at this point, don't you?"

He leaned forward, intertwining his long fingers and resting his chin on them. "Have you come up with something new, then?"

She sat, attempting to make herself comfortable, but it was difficult on the hard cushions of the couch. "I thought we might start by watching the incident again."

His face fell, and he leaned back, sighing with frustration. "No. We've already watched it a hundred times. You won't get anything new from it; we both know that."

"That remains to be seen." Kathleen crossed her arms. He was being impertinent again, like he hadn't been in a long while, and she didn't know why.

"Well, what if you never find anything?"

"Then we'll move on to other procedures. They have some new ones planned for next week to test the sources of the magic in your body." She recognised the look of fear in his eyes and attempted to explain, her words hollow. "You have to understand how valuable you are, Niall; it's not often that a human being is affected by demon magic so powerfully. We stand to learn a lot from you, both about demon and human—"

"I know." He cut her off, looking away in disgust, the muscles in his jaw tightening as he held back his words. "I'm never going to get out of here, am I?"

"You might, eventually. After significant mind reconfiguration." She hated the pain in his eyes. The betrayal. "I'm just being honest with you, Niall. You said that's what you wanted."

"What I wanted." He laughed, his hazel eyes flickering to her as if to share the joke. "Oh, lord." He stared away from her for a long moment, rubbing his face with his hand. "I know it's not your fault," he said. "I know you have your reasons for doing this and—" He paused, glancing up at her again. "—I'm sorry."

"There's no need for you to apologise," she said. "I certainly don't expect sympathy from you. Now, shall we begin?"

He smiled again, more like a grimace, and sat back on the couch, making himself comfortable.

Kathleen let herself take several deep breaths, feeling her walls break down, allowing herself to relax and let her magic flow out of its human shell. She leaned forward, placing her neat, manicured nails on either side of Niall's eyes. He flinched and took a deep breath, letting it out slowly as she plunged in.

They were in a basement. No—a cellar. Kathleen forced herself to remember who she was, separate herself from the memories. She knew this place. She'd seen it before. As Niall had said, a hundred times. She was Niall now, but young Niall, small and skinny and afraid, like he'd been when he had first come to her. But present-Niall was there too, next to her, behind memory-Niall's eyes. He felt resigned, and a little on edge. She didn't know why.

"All right," Niall was saying, in his memory. "Now, here and here's where you say Khireneth. You *must* pronounce it properly. *Khireneth.*"

"Khireneth. Got it. Here and here." Jacky. Kathleen knew that Niall was straining to look at him, even though he couldn't reach beyond the restraints of the memory, and Niall hadn't been looking at him then. He was waiting for the moment when he *had* looked up at Jacky, glanced at his frightened face, not knowing then what he knew now. What Jacky was about to do. The glance passed, only a moment, and Kathleen felt Niall's heart jump for that moment. Lord, did he still love the boy? She wasn't sure. She knew he harboured a fair amount of hate for him as well, but human emotions were tricky to pin down into exact categories like love and hate.

"Good," said memory Niall. "All right, on the count of three. One. Two. Three." Kathleen braced herself for this part; it was difficult to handle, so much dark magic. Her sensibilities as a witch rejected it, told her to run, and it was hard for her to hold on.

Niall, the real Niall, seemed to have shrunk back, content to watch from afar. She didn't blame him, although she'd told him before to keep an eye out for anything notable. She knew he'd probably have had these moments memorised even if he hadn't been forced to watch them over and over again. There was nothing to notice that he hadn't already. Not for her either, but what else was she supposed to do? She'd watch Jacky's—J6's—memory later today too, compare them for differences, attempt to create a three-dimensional image of the scenario. God, that chalky taste in her mouth was nearly overwhelming. She felt herself cough along with Niall as he forced himself to spit the words out, but—Niall hadn't coughed, had he?

She tried to run through her memory of the scenario, to remember if Niall had coughed at that moment before.

He hadn't, had he? Perhaps the memory was breaking down. She coughed again.

Kathleen! She heard a voice calling her name. Niall's voice—adult—not the teenaged memory Niall. He was calling from somewhere behind her, outside the memory. That wasn't possible; he shouldn't be there! How could he have—?

She snapped her head back, attempting to draw herself out of the memory and back onto the couch in Niall's holding room, but she couldn't. Something was keeping her there, rooting her into her mind. The memory and the cellar and the Latin chant were fading away behind her, leaving nothing but her and her feet rooted to the floor, as if trapped in cement. *Kathleen, please don't struggle.*

Niall, what are you doing? she said, forcing herself to keep calm.

I'm sorry, said Niall's voice. She couldn't see him, just hear him talking in her head. *Kathleen, I'm really sorry about this.*

You'll be punished for this, she said. *Niall, I have to punish you for this. I told you when we started you were not to go wandering around in my head, not to change things.*

But I have been, he said. *I have, and you didn't even notice.*

She could feel her eyes widen as she sat on the couch, frozen with her hands glued to Niall's face. *You've been—*

I'm sorry, but yes. I've been looking around in your head for a long time. Whenever you were distracted, looking at my memories, or my magic, I found out I could get in. I know what you know, so— He paused, and Kathleen could feel him drawing back, could feel herself coming back to her body. But something wasn't right. Something was very, very wrong. *I think I've learned how to do this.*

She felt herself breathe and lean back. Her fingers broke contact with Niall, but her mind did not. She saw him blink at her and felt herself tilt her head, confused by the double vision...no, no, it was Niall. Niall was seeing his own eyes through hers, and it was confusing him. She felt herself blink a few times and shook her head, moving her hands down to her lap and breathing deeply. No, no, this was wrong; it wasn't her doing these things. She wanted to resist, wanted to scream at the Sorcerers watching to come and put a stop to this, to save her!

But nothing happened. She sat stock-still, staring into Niall's eyes. *Please don't try to struggle,* he said in her mind. *It won't work.*

What are you going to do? she hissed. At least she was conscious. She could salvage this, somehow. She could talk him down.

I'm sorry, but you can't change my mind. I'm leaving.

They won't let you leave!

Not alone. But they'll let you leave with me.

No! she cried, as she felt her body stand, felt herself lean over to pick up her bag and gesture to Niall, who stood tentatively, looking around the room. He was saying goodbye, she realised, and anger flared up through her. No, goddamn it! She wasn't going to let this happen!

But she didn't have a choice. She walked towards the door, Niall following her, even as he directed her movements. It was terrible, as if he were right behind her eyes, breathing over her shoulder, and she knew he could see everything.

She reached the door, swiping the key card automatically, Niall following close behind her, and for a moment she let herself hope that the Second Hand would know somehow and wouldn't let her out. But he didn't, of course—how could he?—and the door slipped open. They crowded in, uncomfortably close in the small tertiary room, Niall looking down at her with an expression of remorse and pity.

Please, please don't do this. They'll punish me. If you've seen into my mind, you know about my daughter.

He sighed. *I know, and I'm sorry.*

You're sorry! Yes, I'm sure you're sorry, just not sorry enough! You'll let them kill my daughter, an innocent child.

That blood is on their hands, not mine, he said. But they were still linked, and she could feel the guilt eating away at him.

Is your life really more important than hers? Why?

The light glowed green, and the door hissed open. Beyond it stood the Sorcerer and the Second Hand, staring at them in shock.

"There's been a change of plan," she heard her voice say, even as she wanted to scream at them to stop her, stop this, please. "I'm to escort the subject to another holding cell along with J6."

They glanced at each other warily, and then, stupid brainless drones, they both nodded, the Second Hand standing. "I'll go with you," he said, and she felt herself shake her head.

"No, I assure you, the subject is quite sedated. It won't be a problem. Please, keep everything as is."

The Second Hand sat down tentatively. "All right then," he said, and Kathleen swept past him, Niall in tow.

He was barefoot, and she could feel the cold metal of the floor under his feet. They were still connected; it was just that he was in control, and she couldn't shake it. *How long have you been planning this?*

Months. It was partially Jacky's idea. I... I left messages for him, in your head, and him for me.

Messages! Why can't I see them?

I hid them. In your memories. The places you don't like to look at.

She hated him. All good will she'd had for him had dissolved, and she wanted to strap him to one of the torture racks and hack at his mind and his body until he begged for forgiveness. She felt him flinch at the mental image, and then felt his resolve steeling.

That's what's coming for me, isn't it? If I don't get out of here. The rest of my life. They'll never let me go, will they?

I said—

Tell me the truth.

The anger rose up in her like bile. *No, they'd never let you go. Just like they won't let me go. And you don't see me fighting it, do you?*

I'm truly sorry, Kathleen. About Mina—

Don't say her name. Don't even think about her.

I'm sorry, he said again.

Her mind was racing, running through scenarios, trying to think of what to do. *Leave Jacky,* she said suddenly.

What?

If you leave him here, they'll still have someone to study; they'll have use for me. They won't let Mina die. Niall, please.

She could feel his heart breaking. *I'm sorry, Kathleen. I can't.*

Yes, you can! She was seething. *I don't understand how you don't hate him. It's his fault you're in here, you know! It was his choice that brought you here. You should hate him!*

Niall gave a mental head shake. *I don't. I'm sorry. I don't love him anymore. I can't. But I can't hate him. And I can't leave him here either. This was my fault too, and I could never live with myself.*

And what about me? How am I supposed to live with myself?

Please, Kathleen, you're making this harder than it already is.

Good. They had reached Jacky's holding cell. She swiped the key card to let them in, surprising the Sorcerers and Second Hand within. "It's all right," she said. "Orders from higher up: I'm to transport the subjects. You can all go on your lunch breaks."

Why did they listen to her? Couldn't they tell that there was something wrong, that these weren't her orders? But of course they couldn't. They'd been trained to follow orders, to not question. And now the Guild was getting what was coming to it. But of course, she was the one who'd be punished.

I'm sure they won't punish you, said Niall as the Second Hand passed Kathleen, informing her that the subject had quieted down considerably since this morning. Of course he had. *They'll watch your memories, won't they? They'll see it wasn't your fault.*

Tell yourself that if you like.

"Jacky," said Niall out loud, and he ran to the glass, pressing his hands up against it. Jacky sat on the floor in the centre of the room, his head down, his face obscured by the black mats of his hair. "Let him out!" ordered Niall, and Kathleen had no choice but to obey. She went to the controls and manually powered down the whole system, using the last of the residual magic to unlock the two adjacent doors. Jacky's head popped up, inside the holding cell, but the next moment he was standing next to them in the observatory, his eyes wide and angry, his hands reaching for Kathleen's neck.

"Jacky!" shouted Niall, lunging for them and throwing Jacky off her. "Oh god." He pulled Jacky into a tight embrace, which Jacky returned for a moment before turning on Kathleen again.

"What are you waiting for?" he hissed. "We can kill the bitch now!"

"We need her to help us get out still!" cried Niall. "And besides, we're not killing anyone. Jacky! Jacky, *listen to me!*" He'd coloured the words with magical persuasion. Kathleen could feel it rolling off him in waves. The Guild would notice. They'd know. They'd be coming.

Niall glanced at her, his eyes wide. "We've got to go," he said, his voice nearly cracking as he turned back to Jacky, who was hissing and gritting his teeth. "We can talk about this later. We're not *killing* her." He turned to Kathleen. "Take us out of here as quickly as possible."

He was still controlling her. His hold hadn't wavered a bit. God, she *hated* this. She was never going to let it happen again. With a hiss, she swiped the key card, pulling the door open and striding down the now empty hallway, Niall and Jacky in tow. One more swipe of the key card and they were outside, the bright midday sun blinding.

Jacky screamed, and Kathleen could feel the pain in Niall's eyes through their ever-present connection. Five years underground, no sunlight. It was torture. "Where are we?" hissed Jacky, furiously grinding his fist into his eyes and attempting to look around.

"A restricted area in North London," said Niall. "Kathleen, give me your car keys."

"You won't get far," she said, digging into her purse to hand them over. "They'll find you. As soon as you use your magic, they'll find you."

"We won't be using our magic," said Niall.

"You won't be able to escape without it!"

"Haven't you been paying attention, Kathleen?" he said. "We've both been in your head; we know everything that you know. We know witchcraft, untraceable spells, wards to keep from being scried. You'll never find us."

"Oh," she said. "I'll find you."

"We should kill her now." said Jacky, and Niall had to pull him away from her. He was nearly twice as large as Jacky, his muscled body a stark contrast to Jacky's near-atrophied limbs, and he could hold him easily.

"We're not killing her!" he ordered, turning to Kathleen.

"You might as well," she spat.

"I'm just going to put you out," he said. "I'll let you keep your memories, so they know it isn't your fault."

"They won't care," she said, shaking her head slowly. "You know they won't care, you bastard."

"Would you rather we kill you?" asked Jacky with a small smile. "Because unlike you, I'd be glad to do it. Do you remember the way I begged you to kill me, Kathleen? But you said you couldn't. I'll show you how." He took a step towards her, and Niall must have felt the panic well up through her, because he shoved Jacky away and turned to her, pressing his hands roughly to her temples.

"I'm sorry," he said, touching his forehead to hers, and she knew that he was. And she hated it.

I'll find you, she said as she felt him slipping away, felt darkness overtaking her. *I'll find you. Don't you ever stop looking over your shoulder for me.*

No, Kathleen. I never will.

Chapter Three

JUNE, 2013

Thick grey clouds rolled over the fields and gathered on the horizon, creeping steadily upwards to obscure the blue sky, even as the sun burnt bright overhead. It was a strange day. A day for change. Cohen sat staring out the window of the train, his feet pulled up on the seat in front of him and his laptop bag clutched between his knees and his chest, feeling for all the world that he was too young to be on this trip alone.

He brought a finger to his lips to chew the ragged nail there, and then forced himself to draw it away and pull his phone from his pocket instead. He had service still, but he'd made himself downgrade to a plan that didn't include data. He was going to wean himself off the internet if it killed him.

The screen flashed, indicating an incoming message. He ran his finger along the touchscreen automatically. *Hi, bro! Not sure if you're out of service yet but just wanted to say good luck, and call us if u need anything!*

"Us." That was nice. He supposed it was true; his father would likely be more than happy to drive all the way across Ireland just to smile smugly at Cohen and imply that he'd known all along that Cohen was too young and immature to live on his own. His mother would be ecstatic at his return. And Halley...well, Halley was just like Cohen: she'd pretend everything was fine to her last breath. Cohen never had known if she was happy about him going to Witton or not. All she'd ever done was support him. But how strange it felt to be going against the wishes of his parents, of the people he loved. Of anyone, really.

He sighed, leaning back against the scratchy cloth of the train seat and staring out at the countryside. Of course that wasn't true, technically. His family hadn't wanted him to transition. But then he'd had therapists, doctors, years of medical research on his side. This time he had only him, and his gut instinct, and his desire—no, his *need*—to get away. He let the screen go black again, setting the phone down on the seat next to him and closing his eyes. The sound of the train and the hum of the seats was comforting, and he didn't need to reply just yet. For a moment he could just be.

The train pulled into the Witton station a few minutes early, according to his watch. It was a couple minutes after six, and he'd only been riding for a few hours, but already it felt like years since he had woken in his own bed and driven to the train station with Halley and his mother. He'd spoken with his lawyer on the phone before he'd left, and she'd assured him that she would be at the station to pick him up and drive him to the Coughton. It had been as much for his mother's peace of mind as his, but now, stepping off the train onto the station platform, Cohen appreciated the reassurance.

If there was a town nearby, it was very well hidden. The platform was nothing but a block of cement with a weathered metal roof and a long bench. The dirt road in front ran parallel along the train tracks and then veered north over the horizon. Turning in a circle, Cohen could see nothing but green hills peppered with sparse green bushes and trees in every direction, and the rapidly darkening sky. He was glad he'd worn a jumper. Summer was coming, but the cold spring was fighting it every step of the way, and the wind that blew in smelled of thunder and rain.

The small dirt lot next to the station was empty of vehicles, but the train had been early, so Cohen settled in to wait. A quick glance at his phone revealed that he was, at last, out of service. He thought guiltily that he should have messaged Halley back when he'd had the chance. Ah well, he'd call her on the landline when he got there. He wheeled his suitcase over to the metal bench, sat, and wrapped his arms around himself. The wind was picking up and biting, the cold whipping right through his clothes.

Time passed slowly as the clouds rolled in. He remembered the town was south of the station, so he focused on the road to the south, hoping to spot a car. Sandy's tardiness surprised him. She'd always been incredibly professional, and he began to wonder if something had happened to her. He pulled out his phone again to call her before remembering there wasn't any service. Should he try walking to town? Best to wait a little longer first.

He bit his lip, bringing his knees up to his chest and rocking to ward off the cold. This wasn't good. He had no way of contacting anyone, and no idea how to get to town from here, never mind his new house. He stood and began to pace, the cold ripping through his layers of clothes.

Eventually he got up and stood on the bench, hopeful for service up higher. No such luck. Maybe he should try climbing the posts? The mental image of himself doing so would have made him laugh if he weren't beginning to stress so badly. He checked the time on his phone. Nearly an hour had passed!

The wind whirled, the clouds boiled, and a few telltale plunks sounded from the roof. A few seconds later, the rain began in earnest, dropping with greater and greater frequency onto the dust of the road. Cohen stood in the centre of the station, arms crossed against the impending moisture, trying not to panic.

At least he could get his coat out of his case. He bent to open it and managed to keep his things from spilling out as he dug to the bottom for his coat. He paused to touch the plain black medical case that he'd stored carefully in the corner, its presence warming him somewhat. It contained a four-month supply of medical testosterone and the accompanying syringes. The one thing that had finally made him feel human. He'd gladly throw away the entire contents of his suitcase as long as he could hold on to that small black bag.

Well, hopefully that wouldn't be necessary. He managed to extract his coat and stood to pull it on and button it up, his hands beginning to stiffen from the cold. He zipped the suitcase back up quickly, turning as he heard the unmistakable sound of a vehicle.

His relief was short-lived. As the vehicle came to a stop in front of the station, Cohen saw that it was a beat-up blue pickup truck, definitely not the type his lawyer would drive, and the man peering out through the driver's side window was definitely not his lawyer.

Cohen stood cautiously, slinging his laptop bag over his shoulder and stepping towards the truck. The man reached forward and began to roll down the window, flinching from the rain as he did so.

"There isn't a train!" he yelled at Cohen through the deluge.

"What?" Cohen shouted back, unwilling to venture further out into the rain.

"There isn't a train!" the man repeated. "It went by an hour ago, and it only comes by once a day!"

Cohen glanced back at the tracks, before comprehending what the man was saying. "Oh! No, I got *off* the train! I'm waiting for my ride, but she hasn't shown up!"

"Who's your ride, then?"

"Sandy McIntyre? She's my lawyer!"

The man glanced back in the direction he'd come, then turned to look at Cohen again. "Would you like me to give you a ride?" he yelled, gesturing at his truck.

Cohen thought for a moment. It was possible that Sandy was coming and had gotten held up. But it was also entirely possible that he could be waiting here all night. He chewed his lip, staring at the beat-up vehicle and the blurred face of the man who was obviously awaiting his response.

"All right!" he yelled. "Just give me a moment!" He trotted back to grab his suitcase, pulled up the handle, and rolled it to the edge of the platform. The man had already stepped out into the rain and grabbed it for Cohen as he jumped down. "Oh, thank you!"

"It's no problem," the man assured him. "This bloody rain came out of nowhere." He stashed Cohen's bag in behind the passenger seat and then leaned over to unlock the door so Cohen could climb in.

The short jaunt in the rain had left Cohen nearly soaked. He could feel his already curly hair frizzing, drops of water trickling down the curls and into his face. "I look a right mess," he said, bundling his coat around him and glancing at the man next to him.

He was wearing a light jacket with a red button-up underneath. It had a logo on it, so Cohen thought it might be some sort of uniform. He was tall and lean, with long legs and broad shoulders, and his face was angular. His short brown hair was wet from the rain as well, though not as unflatteringly as Cohen's was, and a small goatee accented the rest of his otherwise surprisingly young face. He couldn't have been more than a few years older than Cohen, although Cohen (courtesy of being only a few months into his transition) tended to look much younger than his actual nineteen years.

The man was staring at him curiously. "I know you," he said, and Cohen felt his heart drop. "You make videos on the internet, right? And you write books. Cohen Brandwein."

Relief surged through Cohen. "You used my name," he burst out, immediately becoming embarrassed. "I mean, most people use, you know, the other name. Because I was published under it."

"Right." The man grinned at Cohen as he leaned forward, put the vehicle in gear, and pulled back onto the road. "I saw your video about that. It's rude to use your old name, right?"

"People are rude." Cohen shrugged, sinking into himself. The man had leaned quite close to him, and he smelled good in the rain. Cohen's vestigial uncertainty about his bisexuality was fast dropping with the man's proximity. He supposed he ought to thank him for that.

"Well, I'm not," said the man. "My name's Niall." He held out a hand, and Cohen shook it, feeling a little dazed. "Are you staying in town?"

"Oh, no, at a house called the Coughton. Have you heard of it?"

Niall nodded, squinting a little in the rain. "Yeah, I live right close. Didn't think anyone lived there, though."

"No one does," explained Cohen. "My aunt left it to me when she died a few years ago, and I inherited it on my birthday last month."

"You'll be living there on your own?" Niall glanced at him, eyes raised, and Cohen ducked his head.

"Yeah, well, I sort of wanted to get away."

"I shouldn't lie." Niall looked sheepish. "I saw your video about it. For what it's worth, I'm sorry people are being, y'know, shit to you."

"People aren't being shit to me; well, I mean *most* people aren't. But it's the ones who are that get to you."

"I know the feeling," agreed Niall. "Seriously though, are you going to be okay living there all by yourself? I mean, is anything even hooked up?"

"I'm fine." Cohen couldn't help but laugh at this total stranger's concern. Although he supposed the fact that

Niall had potentially seen all of his videos meant he knew several intimate details of Cohen's life, without Cohen knowing anything about him. It was a weird thought. He always forgot real people saw his videos. He hoped Niall wasn't disappointed by how boring he was in real life. "My lawyer's on it. Or she was supposed to be." He frowned. "She got the electricity and the phone line hooked up, and she was *supposed* to pick me up and—ah, shite."

Niall glanced at him. "What?"

"The key," moaned Cohen. "She was supposed to pick me up, drive me there, and give me the key to get in."

"There's no spare? Rubbish looking for it in this weather, I suppose." Niall squinted out at the rain again. Cohen was surprised he could even see the road through the deluge outside.

"I don't even want to try." Cohen pulled out his phone again, glancing at the screen to confirm its uselessness. "I wish I could just call her."

"Tell you what," said Niall, glancing over at Cohen as he pulled into what looked like a driveway. "Go see if you can get in, and if not, I'll bring you to my place, and you can use my phone."

Cohen heaved a sharp sigh, glancing at Niall. "Thank you," he said. "I really appreciate it. All my plans have gone down the drain today"

"That's the way of things," said Niall with a small smile. "Good luck out there."

"Thanks." Cohen drew his hood up, buttoned the front of his jacket, and then threw himself out into the rain. He trotted as quickly as possible towards the large grey shape that looked like a house, aware that Niall was probably watching him run and wishing he owned a jacket that made him look a bit less like a balloon with legs. He tried not to think about that. The steps were stone, and the water pooled in-between the cracks in his trainers in no time. He hurried to stand under the ledge, pulling his hood back a little as he did so to look around.

The large door was heavy lacquered wood, and the handle was brass. He tried it, not really expecting anything, and his suspicions were confirmed. He was locked out. He turned back to the direction of the truck, lifting his arms in a defeated position, before turning back to the door to try once again for good measure. Nothing.

He looked around. The walls were made of the same stone as the steps, and the only windows he could see were on the second story, above the ledge. Untended flower beds ran along each side of the door, and he didn't much feel like stepping through them, or along the wild growth that was the lawn, to check for a spare key or another opening. It was ridiculous to think it wouldn't have been locked up tightly anyway. The only person here in years had been Sandy, and she...well, he'd *thought* she was reliable. Maybe not.

He hurried back to the truck as quickly as possible, attempting futilely to brush off some of the rain before ducking back onto the seat.

"No luck?" asked Niall, and Cohen shook his head.

"I mean, if you wouldn't mind taking me back to town, I'm sure I can get a room there." He shook his arms, effectively spraying water all over the dash and seats. "I'm really sorry about this."

"It's not a problem." Niall seemed much more amused than annoyed. "If you want to go into town, I can bring you there, but my place is like five minutes away. You can stay there. Really."

Cohen bit his lip. "I-I'd *like* to, but I don't want to impose."

"Trust me, you won't be imposing. I like to entertain."

"Do you entertain a lot?" asked Cohen as they pulled out of the driveway, and Niall laughed.

"I wish. You'll find the locals are a pretty tight-knit group. They don't welcome strangers easily."

"Well, that's probably a good thing. I'm supposed to be writing, not canoodling with the natives."

Niall snorted. "Are you going to write the next one in the series, then?"

"Oh, god, you've read them." Cohen leaned forward to hide his face between his knees, and Niall laughed again.

"I said I did, didn't I?"

"They're so bad. They're—I wrote them when I was sixteen. How would you like to have something you wrote when you were sixteen published?"

"I thought they were good."

"Well, they're fine, but..." Cohen straightened up again, letting out a long, frustrated moan. "They're just not what I would write now. Not at all, and that's why I'm having trouble writing the next one."

"So write something completely different," said Niall with a shrug.

"But people want the next one. You just asked me about the next one."

"Well, yeah, but screw what I want. Write what you want to write."

"Yeah." Cohen leaned on his fist, staring out at the rain. "It's easy when you say it like that."

★

Niall carried Cohen's luggage for him, much to Cohen's never-ending thanks. They made a mad dash for the house and managed to get in without drowning. Cohen stood shivering on the porch while Niall hurriedly unlocked the door.

It was blissfully warm and dry inside, but Cohen barely noticed, too preoccupied with the contents of the house.

"What is all this stuff?" he asked, turning in circles and staring at the rows and rows of strings hanging from the ceiling and walls. They were draped over openings and doorways, lined under windows, even along the floor on either side of the hallway, and from all of them hung all manner of strange things. Dried plants mostly, and roots and beads and unlit candles. The smell of them was at the same time musky and delicious, and Cohen almost felt light-headed.

"Well," said Niall, once again looking a little sheepish as he locked the door and tied a string of beads across the entrance. "I'm sort of a witch."

"You're sort of a witch," repeated Cohen, gawking at Niall. He didn't know whether to be impressed or terrified or strangely turned on. "I'm Jewish, you know."

Niall bit his lip, looking just a little wicked. "Are you going to stone me?"

"No, we don't do that anymore," said Cohen, looking around the house again, distracted. "What's it all for?"

"Protection, mostly. Good luck, that sort of thing."

"It's a little extreme isn't it?" Cohen glanced at Niall, who was looking a little guilty.

"Suppose so. Now you see why I don't entertain much. Kitchen's this way."

The house was small, and only one storey high. Cohen could only see a few rooms down the hall. The kitchen and the sitting room were only one room. The floor was linoleum, the carpet old, and the wallpaper peeling. Despite all that, it was warm and comfortable. Niall turned on the dim light and lit a few candles. He opened the blinds in the sitting room to reveal large bay windows, currently assaulted by the heavy rain, and closed them again with a *tsk*.

"No service," he said, tossing a sleek cordless phone to Cohen. It seemed strangely out of place amongst the aged browns and greens of the decor. "You can try to call your lawyer on that though."

"Thanks." Cohen sat on the ageing couch, undid the laces on his now soaked trainers, and pulled them off before he dialled Sandy's number. It rang five times, then went to voicemail. He left Sandy a message explaining what had happened and requesting she call him back. Then there was nothing else to do. "Are you sure you're all right with me staying here?" he asked Niall.

"It's not a problem at all," Niall assured him. "Just let me get changed and make up the spare room."

He left, and Cohen called Halley to let her know what had happened.

"Oh, Cohen, good! Mam was starting to get worried! Is everything all right?"

"Sort of." Cohen leaned back on the couch, allowing himself to relax for the first time since the rain had started. "Sandy never showed up at the station, though."

"What? Where are you, then?"

Cohen explained everything to her as Niall came back into the room. He had changed into a pair of jeans and a light T-shirt. His body looked amazing, and Cohen almost forgot what he was saying to Halley.

"You mean you got into a car with a man you don't know, and now you're at his *house*?" Halley was nearly whispering. "That is *so* not safe! What am I supposed to tell Mam and Dad?"

"That I'm *fine,* Halley; just tell them a nice man is letting me stay with him."

"Cohen, just because you're a guy now doesn't mean it's safe to go home with strange men. And anyway, what if he knows who you are, and he knows that you're really—" Cohen flinched, and it was almost as if Halley could hear it over the phone. "I'm sorry, but why do you have to make us worry about you?"

"It's not really my fault," said Cohen, a little crosser than he wanted to be. "I did have everything planned out, but things went wrong. Anyway, I can't go through life not trusting anybody."

"You're just stupidly optimistic is all," said Halley, sighing. "All right, I'll tell Mam and Dad you're fine, and *call me* in the morning, and tell this bloke you're staying with that you're going to, okay?"

"I will, okay?"

"What's he like anyway? Is he old?"

"What? No."

"Is he, you know, hot?"

"Um." Cohen cleared his throat. "He's in the room."

"Oh!" Halley giggled. "Okay then, fine. I'll leave you to that. And call me when you get to your place, all right?"

"I will. I'll call you in the morning, and I'll call you when I've got to the Coughton, and also when I've brushed my teeth. I'll be fine, Halley."

"Well, you're my little sis—" She cut off with an intake of breath, and Cohen flinched violently. Niall, who had gone into the kitchen to put the kettle on, glanced at Cohen, looking concerned.

It's okay, Cohen mouthed at him. The line was silent.

"I'm really sorry," said Halley, sounding wretched. "Cohen, I'm really sorry, okay? I just forgot."

"I know." Cohen nodded, trying to breathe. "It's fine, really, Halley. I appreciate that you're trying."

"I am trying," she said. "Really, I am."

Niall took a step into the living room. "Do you want me to go?" he asked, and Cohen shook his head.

"It's okay." Cohen forced a smile into his voice. "You're *my* sister, so I can't be mad at you."

"Yeah, right." Halley gave a forced laugh. "Okay, *call* me tomorrow, kid. You hear me?"

"I will," he said. "I promise."

"G'night, little brother."

"Goodnight."

He hung up the phone, leaning back against the couch and breathing slowly. His tolerance for being misgendered had gone down now that it wasn't happening all the time. When it had happened all the time, it had just been like a slow-burning, unidentifiable sickness. Now every "he" was a relief, and every "she" and "sister," every mention of his birth name, was like a punch to the gut. He hated it.

"Are you okay?" asked Niall, looking concerned as he pulled a couple of mugs from the cupboard and began to make tea. "What happened?"

"Just..." Cohen put a hand to his face. "I can't really explain. Nothing, really. She's worried about me, of course. Spending the night with a strange man."

"I am a little strange," said Niall, glancing at his magical mobiles. He sounded a little sad about that. Wistful.

"I don't think so," said Cohen. "Even if you are, I'm pretty sure it's fashionable these days."

That brought a laugh from Niall. "I'll make you dinner," he said. "I'm sorry, but I'm a vegetarian, so you might not like anything I have."

"Ah." Cohen fretted. He wished he weren't such a picky eater. "Vegetarian sounds good?"

"You say that now," said Niall with a laugh. "Oh, cream or sugar?"

"Both please," said Cohen. "Why are you a vegetarian?" he asked, turning to watch Niall as he left the tea to steep and produced a package of tofu and some vegetables from the fridge. "Is it like a health thing? I mean, you look pretty fit." He flushed, wishing he could eat his words for dinner. "I mean you look *healthy*. You know what? Just ignore everything I say for the rest of the night."

Niall laughed as he turned the stove on and poured a bottle of dark sauce into a pan. "I could probably get in better shape if I ate meat," he admitted. "It's hard to put on weight eating tofu but—" He paused, wrestling momentarily with the package. "I just can't. I'm a big softie, I suppose, and once you really look into what they do to the animals—" He smiled, glancing at Cohen. "Well, I won't go into it."

"I suppose it's just one of those things," said Cohen, trying desperately to be tactful. "I don't really like to think about it because if I did I'd have to stop eating meat."

"Mm." Niall paused again, returning to the fridge to grab a clove of garlic. "Everyone has different things. You know, things you ignore because if you let yourself feel guilty, or angry about every little thing that you should..."

"It would kill you," finished Cohen. "But everyone's got a few things they can't ignore, right? Causes."

"Don't know if tofu is a cause," chuckled Niall, and Cohen laughed. Niall finished making the tea and tossed the bags in the bin, bringing Cohen's mug into the living room for him. "So what's yours? Your cause, I mean."

Cohen took a sip of his tea, thinking. "Suppose like LGBT stuff," he said. "It's hard to ignore when you are, you know."

"I don't know about that." Niall left the food to simmer in the pan, coming to sit next to Cohen with his tea. "I've pretty much managed to, but I don't suppose I've ever really had to come out to anyone."

Cohen's heart nearly leapt into his throat at the prospect of Niall being gay, but he forced it down quickly. He was feeling anxious, and that constant doubtful voice was eating away at him.

"Are you okay?" asked Niall. "Did I say something wrong?"

"No," said Cohen. "Sorry." He tried to force his heart rate down, to no avail. There was no way to explain it really. "Another thing I can't talk about."

Niall was quiet for a moment. "Can't talk about or don't want to talk about? Because you don't need to censor yourself. I promise I won't be, like, weirded out or anything. I like to hear...about people. I didn't get a lot of contact with people for a long time when I was younger."

Cohen rubbed his face, wondering how to explain what he was feeling, or if he even wanted to. "It's stupid; it's got nothing to do with what we were talking about, really." Well, that was a lie. But he didn't want to explain the connection to Niall. He took another sip of his tea, thinking, and then blurted out, "You ever feel like no one will ever want to be with you? Like because of the choices you made, out of necessity even, you're destined to be alone forever?"

The words hung heavy in the air. Cohen flinched at himself. He hadn't meant it to come out so depressing.

Niall nodded though. "Yeah," he said. "You think because you're transitioning that no one will want to be with you?"

"Well." Cohen leaned back on the couch, surprised by Niall's straightforwardness. "I guess I do. I mean, I know bi people exist, and plenty of trans people have partners, I *know* that, but I can't help feeling like anyone who likes girls won't like how I look, and anyone who likes boys won't like how I...ah." He blushed. "This is about to get kind of explicit. I think I should stop."

"I think," said Niall, setting his tea on the coffee table and leaning closer to Cohen, "that if you're going to date someone, you should date someone who likes boys."

"That'd certainly be better for my mental health," agreed Cohen, sighing. "But I can't help feeling they'd be disappointed."

"I don't think you're giving us enough credit," said Niall with a small smile. "We care about more than just cocks, you know."

Cohen laughed and bit back what he wanted to say, which was *why would any man want me?* "Thanks," he said instead. "See, you've done your part to fight stereotypes about gay men."

"Fighting for the cause," laughed Niall, and he got up again to check the food. The couch shifted as he stood, and Cohen felt stupidly like they'd just had a rather intimate moment. Spoiled by his awkwardness, of course, but what wasn't?

"I've made you a stir-fry," said Niall. "It isn't amazing, but it's weeknight cooking; what can I say?"

"Where do you work?" asked Cohen, getting up to bring the tea mugs to the table.

"Just the little corner shop in town." Niall plated the dinner expertly and placed it in front of Cohen, who looked at it dubiously. "It's a job."

"Did you grow up in town?" asked Cohen, and Niall shook his head, spearing a piece of tofu on his fork and eating quickly. "So, why did you move here then?"

Niall took another bite and was quiet as he chewed. Cohen dutifully copied him, taking a bite out of a pepper. Niall had cooked the vegetables and tofu in a teriyaki and garlic sauce which made it surprisingly tolerable.

"Actually, I just came here to get away, same as you," said Niall finally, getting up to procure a jug of water and glasses. "I only moved here a few months ago," he explained, sitting down and pouring the water. "I think I mentioned the locals haven't warmed to me yet. So, are you going to get a lot of writing done at the Coughton?"

Cohen blinked, surprised at how quickly Niall had turned the conversation back to him. Usually that was Cohen's tactic. "I *hope* so. I want to write my next book."

"Hmm." Niall took another bite of tofu. "I hope you write a new book."

"I thought you wanted me to finish the series!"

"I changed my mind. I'm allowed to change my mind."

"Right," said Cohen. "Well, I have a contract for the next one, and I do have to make money eventually."

"That's not very artistic of you," said Niall.

"Oh, shut up!" Cohen couldn't help but laugh. Niall was pushing his buttons, but it felt more like flirting than teasing. At least, he hoped it was. "You're so rude! You're the rudest person I've ever imposed on and made feed me dinner."

"I imagine so," laughed Niall. "So, if you just give me a moment to clear out the spare bedroom after this, you can sleep in there."

"That'd be great," said Cohen. "Really, thanks again."

"It's no problem," Niall reassured him. "I like guests."

★

Cohen waited until Niall had said goodnight and disappeared into his bedroom before sneaking into the toilet. It was small, with a yellowed tub and sink, and was stocked with only the most basic necessities: a comb, razor, soap, and some cheap shampoo. Cohen was lucky he had packed along all of his toiletries. He had far too many, but he was convinced that giving up his femininity did not have to mean giving up nice soap.

He turned to undress in front of the mirror, only then to notice it had been covered with an opaque white sheet. Cohen stared at it for a moment, wondering if the mirror under it was broken. It seemed an odd thing to do, to cover a mirror, but he supposed he was staying in a house with strings of magical plants hung everywhere (even over the toilet). He shivered. Only a covered mirror. Why did that make him so uncomfortable?

His fingers brushed the soft cloth as he reached forward to pull it aside. The glass was shiny and unbroken. His own face stared back at him, his eyes a little wider than normal, and his dark hair unimaginably frizzy. His reflection narrowed his eyes at him, pinching his mouth to the side and wrinkling his nose. "You look terrible," he told himself under his breath. "Stop freaking out, and get in the shower."

He tugged his clothes off and then, paranoid, checked to make sure the door was locked one more time before struggling to pull his binder over his head. He crossed his arms in front of himself automatically, suddenly glad the mirror was covered, and fingered the raw callouses under his armpits. He'd gained weight lately, and the binder was too tight on him, but he couldn't bring himself to buy a bigger size.

Well, maybe he'd just switch to eating tofu and peppers like Niall. It seemed to work wonders on him.

He sighed, distancing himself from his body as well as he could, and stepped into the tub, pulling the plastic curtain shut and turning the water on. It was blissfully warm. He hadn't realised how chilled he'd been from the rain.

Not entirely comfortable in the old, unfamiliar shower, he washed and towelled off as fast as possible before changing into his pyjamas. Then, with his things clutched as tightly as possible to his chest, he raced to the spare bedroom, shut the door behind him, and jumped into the bed. He left the binder on the floor next to the bed so he could put it on first thing in the morning.

He was drifting off before he remembered he hadn't even plugged his phone in for the night. Not that it really mattered, but he couldn't remember the last time he had gone to sleep without it next to him. Perhaps he wasn't quite as addicted as he'd thought though, because he had no trouble falling deep into the soft scratchiness of the bed, the smell of dust and dried plants surprisingly comforting, and the sound of the rain the same as it always had been, lulling him into oblivion.

He awoke from his dreams reluctantly. He'd been dreaming of relief, of a world where everything was under his control. It was unusual for him to have such dreams, and he didn't want to wake. But the sound of a loud knock at the door, and then the door slamming and harsh voices shouting dragged him upwards. He opened his eyes and sat up, listening to make sense of the noises.

The covers fell from his chest, and he clutched his arms to cover himself. Something was wrong. He threw himself out of bed, reaching down to scoop up his binder and pulling his pyjama shirt off in the same motion. The morning chill bit at his bare skin as he tugged his clothes on and rushed out into the kitchen.

"Cohen." Niall was standing in the middle of his kitchen, surrounded by police, their neon yellow-and-navy uniforms too bright and cold for the warmth of the house. His hair was messy, and his eyes red-rimmed and frightened. "You should go back to the bedroom," he said, sounding tired but urgent.

Cohen stayed rooted to the spot. "What's going on?"

"Do you know this man?" asked one of the Gardai, a tall, broad woman with frizzy orange hair. She turned to look at Cohen, eyeing him critically.

"Not really," said Cohen. "He just gave me a place to stay last night." What was going on? He had to get his mind working properly. Everything was moving too quickly, blurry somehow.

The woman stepped towards him, coming between Cohen and Niall. "What's your name, lad?" she asked, a touch of softness in her voice.

"It's Cohen," said Cohen, his heart skipping a beat.

"Cohen," she repeated. "It's very important that you cooperate with us, Cohen, and that you tell us everything."

Cohen nodded, swallowing.

"Leave him alone," said Niall, and the woman turned to look at him. "I don't know what's going on, but he has nothing to do with it."

"Cohen," said the woman again, and Cohen looked back to her. "What are you doing here? Why did you spend the night here?"

"I...I..." Niall was looking at Cohen, some desperate look in his eyes, but Cohen couldn't tell what it meant for the life of him. Did Niall want him to lie? What were the police doing here? "I was supposed to be picked up at the train station by my lawyer, but she never showed up. Niall drove by, and—and it was raining, so he offered to drive me home, but then I couldn't get into my place because I didn't have my key..." he trailed off, unsure of what the Garda wanted to hear.

"What's your lawyer's name?"

"Sandy McIntyre. I just moved into town. She was going to meet me and bring me to the house, but she never showed up."

"I see." The Garda was quiet for a moment. "Around what time were you picked up from the station?"

"I-I guess it was..." Cohen thought for a moment, remembered looking at his phone and thinking that Sandy was an hour late. "Maybe a little after seven?"

Niall's eyes widened in what Cohen thought was sudden relief.

"Hmm," said the Garda. "Would you be willing to swear that in a court of law?"

Cohen felt a spurt of adrenaline shoot through him. "Yes, of course. Why? What's going on?"

She signalled to the other four Gardai, who moved forward to turn Niall around and cuff his hands. Cohen stared, disbelieving, and the Chief Garda turned to him again. "Sandy McIntyre is dead," she explained. "And this man is our primary suspect."

Chapter Four

Cohen was in shock the entire way to the Garda station. He had spent the night in the house of a murderer? Had Halley been right? He hadn't called her. He needed to call her and let her know he was okay. He shuddered at the thought that he might not have been.

He felt sick. He'd been so personal last night with Niall. Told him things about himself, eaten his food. He wanted to ask the Garda in the driver's seat a million questions, but the man told him everything would be explained at the station.

He didn't see Niall again until after he had been questioned extensively about the previous day twice, once by a Garda and then again by a criminal lawyer. Only then was the situation explained to him. The Chief Garda (her name was Myrna) introduced herself to him properly and thanked him for his cooperation. Cohen, tired from the stress of being questioned, and feeling horribly dysphoric from having to sign his birth name on several forms, was less friendly than he normally would have been, but she didn't seem to mind.

"You may well have saved that young man from prison," she told Cohen. "You're his only alibi."

"Please just tell me what happened," sighed Cohen, wishing for his bed back in Dublin. He'd been able to speak to Halley on the phone briefly when they had arrived at the station, with only enough time to explain everything succinctly, and he knew he had sounded terrible. No doubt Halley had told their parents everything, and they were worried sick about him. He felt horrible for leaving and then for getting involved in something so terrifying, even though it hadn't been his fault. He wondered if maybe he should just go back to Dublin.

"Sandy McIntyre's body was found at eight o'clock this morning by her co-worker who went to check on her when she didn't turn up at work," said Myrna as she rifled through her papers, organizing them into folders. "There is video surveillance of a man that looks very much like your friend Niall, walking into the apartment complex where she lives at exactly 7:14 p.m. the night before. Since he finished work at seven o'clock last night, it seemed very plausible that it was him."

"But, it can't have been," said Cohen breathlessly, "because I was with him then; he was picking me up at the station."

"Precisely," said Myrna. "Furthermore, as you've stated, Sandy had plans to pick you up from the train station at six o'clock, correct? But she never showed, which suggests that the murder took place before six o'clock, when Niall was still accounted for at work."

Cohen breathed a deep sigh, letting his head fall back onto the cold leather of his chair. "So he didn't do it." He felt like he was going to collapse into a pile of debris.

"It doesn't seem likely." Myrna tsked and turned away, slipping the folders into a drawer and locking it. "Not the first time I've been wrong."

Cohen tore his eyes away from the dusty ceiling fan to look back at her. "You thought it was him?"

Myrna got up, pulling on her heavy uniform coat and slinging her bag over her shoulder. "Well, to be perfectly honest, everyone did."

"Isn't that a little harsh?"

Myrna shrugged, but she stepped closer to him and leaned against her desk, shoving her hands into her pockets. "I'm not saying it's right," she said. "Just that it's what everyone, including me, thought. I know everyone in this town. I don't like to think that any of them are murderers, and three murders in the four months since a new face arrives in town does arouse suspicion—"

"Wait." Cohen gripped the arms of his chair. "Three murders? You mean this isn't—"

"The first?" finished Myrna. "Not the first like this. I'm sorry, I forgot you didn't know. Everyone in town knows about them. There was a little girl, five years old, and then a man. Now Sandy. The victims are all killed in the same way, so we know we're dealing with a serial killer. I'm sorry. You look pale."

"It's just—" Cohen could feel his insides curling up. "I might not have moved here if I'd known."

Myrna nodded. "The thought was to keep it from going to large presses because these kinds of killers like publicity. I'm sorry. If you like, I can put you back on a train to Dublin."

Cohen thought about how his parents would react. They'd never let him live on his own again. He didn't want to go back to Dublin, anyway. He really didn't. "I want to stay here." He took a deep breath. "But I need to be able to get into my house."

Myrna nodded, looking around as if she was thinking. "We recovered most of her things for evidence," she explained. "I'll see if I can get you your key."

"Thanks," said Cohen as she started towards the door to her office. "Um."

Myrna turned to look back at him.

"What will happen to Niall?"

"He'll be tried out of court in a few weeks. The attorney will set a bail, and he'll be kept here until someone pays it."

"Will someone?"

She shrugged. "It would seem he doesn't have any family."

"But won't he miss work?"

"Are you suggesting I pay it?" she asked, her stare hard.

"Well I—" Cohen swallowed. "I mean, how much is it?"

"I'd have to ask the attorney, but probably a couple of thousand."

"But he didn't *do* anything."

"That hasn't been proven in court yet."

"He'll lose his job."

"I'm sorry"—Myrna shrugged—"but I don't have an extra two thousand quid. I have children to feed."

Cohen was going to get in trouble with his parents for doing this. Even though the money was technically his now that he was an adult, they'd always kept a tight leash on him, ever since he'd been paid for his first book. They didn't want him spending it all on frivolous things. But this wasn't frivolous. "I have it," he said. "I'll pay."

Myrna got him his key and drove them both home in her cruiser. On the way, she questioned Niall again, asking him if he had any enemies who might have wanted to set him up. The video, she explained, was of someone who looked very much like Niall, down to the clothes. It seemed too much of a coincidence to ignore.

"I don't know," said Niall. "I told them everything I know. I just want to go home." He hadn't spoken much at all, save to thank Cohen for paying his bail and Myrna for driving him home. Cohen didn't really blame him. He was exhausted himself, and he hadn't just been accused of murder.

They stopped at Niall's place first, to grab Cohen's things and drop Niall off. Myrna accompanied them both inside, so he didn't have a chance to talk to Niall privately. He collected his things awkwardly from the spare room, and thanked Niall on his way out. Niall was quiet, but as they drove away, he saw Niall in the window, looking out after them.

When they pulled into the driveway at the Coughton, Cohen had a chance to look at it for the first time properly. It looked ancient. The stone walls were covered in crawling green ivy, and its high square windows were dark and murky. An old, boxy car sat in the driveway next to it, and Cohen glanced at the keychain that Myrna had acquired for him to confirm that a small matching ignition key accompanied the much more antiquated house key. At least he'd have transport. It felt weird to be living in his deceased aunt's house, driving her car. But she had left it all to him.

"You're going to be okay here?" Myrna asked him as she helped him carry his things to the door over the still-wet grass. There had been a stone walkway at one point, but it had nearly grown over in the two years of unoccupancy. The doorknob and lock were ornate copper, covered in a green patina, and the key matched. Cohen placed the heavy key in and turned it, feeling the weights shift inside. There was a *thunk* and the door unlocked. He turned the handle, slightly more shiny from use, and pushed the heavy wooden door open.

Inside, it was dark and dry. Cohen leaned forward, smelling dust and stagnancy. He stepped in, feeling a heavy rug under his shoes, and looked around. There was a tarnished silver switch on the wall, circular with matching wire running up to the ceiling. When he flipped it, a soft yellow glow illuminated the room, better than the sunlight from the dusty windows.

"Well, there's electricity, so I should be okay," he told Myrna, ducking back outside to grab his bag. "I'll drive the car into town tomorrow and stock up."

"You've got enough food for tonight, then?" she asked, and he nodded. He'd brought a few cans of beans and soup with him from home, suspecting the house would be empty. She nodded, seeming satisfied. "I'd like to invite you to dinner sometime," she said, pulling a notebook from her breast pocket and scribbling her number down. "My daughter's a big fan of yours; she'd love to meet you."

Cohen was too shocked to respond for a moment. He hadn't even realised Myrna knew who he was. "Of course," he said, when he found his voice again. "I'd like that."

Myrna shoved her hands in her pockets, glanced behind him into the dim foyer, and nodded once again. "Make sure you lock your doors," she said. "Have a good night."

Cohen watched her walk back to the car and get in. As the car drove away down the worn road, he suddenly felt very alone.

He stepped into the foyer of the house once again and shut the door behind him. It took a moment for his eyes to adjust to the dimness, as if the house were hiding its secrets from him, only giving them up reluctantly. He pulled his coat around himself, glad he was wearing it. First order of business was to find a thermostat, although the grey stone walls didn't look like they would hold heat well.

He took a few steps forward, the fabric of the rug swallowing his footsteps. The foyer was two stories, the only windows high above the doorway. Craning his neck, Cohen could just see the wooden rafters above. The light came from an old electric chandelier, dull, painted gold glinting amongst cobwebs. He'd have to find a ladder and clean it up.

He walked through the house, opening doors and turning on light switches, hoping it would make the place a little warmer. If not for the dust and darkness, he could almost imagine his aunt still lived here. They'd visited when he and Halley were children until his mother had decided that the house was unsafe for children. It appeared that his aunt's hoarding tendencies had increased in the years following.

The couches in the sitting room were covered in white sheets, but he didn't bother to remove them yet. He slipped into the dining room, ran his hand along the dusty white cloth covering the large table, and examined the vast collection of china in the cabinet. He didn't think he'd ever be able to make himself eat in here.

Luckily the kitchen was a little cosier. The floor was mint-green tile, the ceiling low, and a small, more modern table sat in the centre with a few chairs around it. Cohen opened the old, squat fridge to check that it worked, and closed it again, shivering. The cupboards were empty, of course—cleared out, although all manner of knick-knacks and garbage lay strewn about and pushed to the back of the counters. The dust made everything eerie and grey.

A small window was set next to a wooden door leading outside, and he walked towards it, slid his sleeve over his fist, and rubbed away some of the condensation and murk. When he did, a bit of light shone through, illuminating the room, although the grey sky was darkening quickly. He'd need to clean the windows. That would make everything much less dreary. Hopefully it wouldn't rain again the next day, although anything would be better than the grey of today.

He shivered again, looking around for a thermostat. But there was nothing, only two more rooms filled to the brim with covered furniture, and boxes and boxes of junk. Then beyond, he spotted what looked like a ballroom or a music room with an elaborately tiled floor and long velvet curtains in front of tall glass windows. The paint on the high, gilded ceiling was chipping, and the whole room smelled of decay and disuse. Cohen shivered and left quickly, returning to his case near the front door and starting up the grand staircase.

If he had to guess, he'd say his aunt had done a lot more living upstairs. There was another, smaller sitting room, and the guest rooms he remembered staying in when he'd visited with his family. The sitting room had an old, boxy television, and a phone that had a dial tone when he picked up. A giant golden menorah sat on the mantel above the fireplace. He'd always been afraid of it falling on him as a child, but now it felt familiar and comforting.

At last, he found the bedroom. In the corner, by yet another fireplace, sat an enormous, decrepit space heater with a dark faux-wood finish. He found the plug and fitted it into the socket, another tarnished silver block with a metal cable connecting it to the other outlets and lights in the house. He pressed the buttons on the top experimentally.

A dim orange light began to glow, and the heater made a noise like the engine of a dying, old car, followed by a high-pitched whirring. Cohen coughed, stepping back as a puff of dust emanated from it, along with the overpowering smell of burning and, mercifully, a gradual spread of heat.

He knelt for a minute, warming his hands, before the smell became overwhelming, and he stood, coughing, and turned away. He rolled his suitcase over to the bed and pulled the white sheet off, leaving it in a heap on the floor. The mattress was bare, but he quickly found the bedding in the closet. His aunt's clothes were still there, thanks to the order in her will that everything be left for Cohen.

She'd been so proud that he'd published a book. He wondered if she'd have been as proud if she'd known about his transition.

Luckily, the stiff, old sheets didn't smell like anything except detergent and dust. He reminded himself that his aunt had died in a hospital, not here in her bed, but it was still creepy. He pulled the sheets over the bed and spread the thick embroidered comforter, tucking the edges in.

He shivered again. The heater was warming the room slowly, but he didn't feel ready to take his coat off. It was dark, strangely so. He went to the window, pulling the heavy curtains away and wiping the window to let more of the light in. Directly below him was the garden he'd seen out the kitchen window, the hedges and bushes overgrown. It looked like there was a vegetable patch as well. Maybe he could grow vegetables if he was still here come fall. His stomach growled at the thought of vegetables—he must really be hungry. The only thing he'd eaten all day was a sandwich provided for him at the police station. He definitely needed to have dinner.

He opened his case and pulled out one of the tins of beans he'd brought along as well as a few juice boxes. It was enough to last him until tomorrow, when he could take the car into town and do some proper shopping. He trotted downstairs and turned the oven on, opening it to allow it to heat the place up. How his aunt had ever managed to live there through the winters was beyond him, although he supposed he might have to find out. Maybe he just hadn't found the thermostat yet, but he doubted the place had central heating.

He had just finished washing a pot and had finally found a can opener when there was a heavy, insistent knock on the door. He stopped, pulling the can away from the machine and listening. The knock came again, three times in quick succession.

For a brief second, he thought it must be Sandy, and the thought made his empty stomach queasy. He wiped his hands off on the dishtowel and shut the oven door before venturing into the foyer. He wished the door had a peephole, or at least that the only windows weren't so high up. Myrna had told him to keep the door locked, but that wouldn't do any good if he opened the door for a—no—*the* murderer.

The knock came again. "Who is it?" he called, his voice coming out much more childish and high-pitched than he wanted it to.

"It's Niall. Cohen, you have to let me in; it's important."

Niall. Cohen's heart jumped with excitement at seeing him again. This was ridiculous. Was he thirteen again? He unlocked the door and pulled it open. Niall stood on his doorstep, looking flushed. He was wearing the same clothes from this morning, and he was carrying a large suitcase.

"Hi," he said, and Cohen was sure he was imagining that Niall's eyes lit up at the sight of him. "Hi, Cohen. I'm glad you're okay."

"Of course I'm okay," said Cohen, stepping aside to let Niall in. "You just saw me an hour ago."

"I know." Niall was looking around the foyer, his eyes a little frantic. "I had to go home and get some stuff, but I'm here now. Cohen." He looked Cohen in the eye, his expression deadly serious. "You're not going to like me very much for this; in fact, you're probably going to think I'm crazy, but you have to let me do this."

"What?" asked Cohen, and Niall knelt to open the suitcase. It was full to the brim with dried plants and amulets. He wasn't sure if Niall had strung more, or simply taken the ones in his house down. "What are those for?" Cohen asked warily.

"Protection," said Niall, sighing determinedly as he began to pull long strings of them out of the case. He looked around the foyer with a calculating expression. "We'll have to use these sparingly. Show me the exits."

"Um, no." Cohen crossed his arms and stared at Niall. Half of him was completely weirded out, and the other half wanted to laugh. "You're not putting those things all over my house. I'm trying to make the place look *better*."

"I have to."

"Why?"

Niall stared at him, and his jaw tightened a little. "Protection."

Cohen was trying and failing to keep the smile off his face. "Niall, it's fine if you want to practise your religion in your own house, but I'm not okay with you bringing it here, no matter how good your intentions are."

Niall seemed to smile a little despite himself. Maybe an automatic response to Cohen's. "You're suddenly so eloquent."

"Well, I'm tired, and I need to eat. You're welcome to"—he gestured flippantly at the kitchen—"come have beans with me."

Niall didn't move. "It's not a religion," he said. "It's a practice."

"Okay, whatever, practise it at home." Cohen turned and headed back to the kitchen, partly because he was starving and partially to break Niall's intense eye contact. Niall followed him though.

"I can't," he said as Cohen grabbed the can of beans and attempted to work the rusty old can opener. "You have protections on you, so I can't do magic directly to you; I have to place it around you."

"What are you *talking* about?" Cohen turned back to Niall. The humour was beginning to wear thin. How could he not have noticed this whole time that Niall was a little odd? He'd seemed like such a normal, harmless pagan.

Niall's voice was soft and insistent, his face pleading. "Cohen, you're looking at me like I'm crazy, but I promise I'm not. I'm telling the truth. Is it that hard to believe that magic exists and I can do it?"

Cohen turned away again to grab the pot and place it on the stove. "Um, I'm sane, so *yes*."

"Then believe this," said Niall, his voice becoming sharper. "I'm sorry that I got you involved in this, but when you helped me today, you attracted the attention of the man who killed Sandy McIntyre and two other people. You're not safe anymore."

Cohen suddenly wished he hadn't taken off his coat. He shivered and dropped the pan on the stove, turning back to face Niall. "You know who did it?" he hissed. "You know, and you didn't tell the police?"

"I couldn't," Niall said, his brow knitted. "I can't let people know." He sighed, looking away, and Cohen could see the tightness in his cheek again. "It's very complicated, and I can explain everything, but please let me put these protections up first."

Cohen turned back to the stove. His mind was a whirl, his whole body on high alert. "I don't believe you."

"I can prove it," said Niall. "If I prove it, will you let me?"

"Prove what?"

"That I can do magic."

Cohen couldn't help but laugh, although there was little humour in it. "Sure, whatever."

Niall stepped closer to him and uncrossed his arms, holding a hand out. Cohen forced himself not to back away. "Can I see that?" Niall asked, gesturing at the open can of beans that Cohen had picked up.

Cohen handed him the can reluctantly. He'd thought Niall was the only one in town he could trust. Now it seemed more and more like he was the craziest person he'd met so far.

Niall took the can and cupped it in his hands, staring down at it. He said a few words in something that sounded like Russian. For a second, nothing happened. Then there was a loud pop, and beans shot up out of the can, catapulting all over the kitchen. Cohen, who had flinched and turned away at the noise, uncovered his face hesitantly and stared at Niall, who was looking sheepish.

"Ah, that was probably too big a spell for that size," said Niall, looking down at the can. "But look, it's hot!"

It was indeed. Steam was rising from the beans that were left in the can, and Niall was holding it gingerly, as if the metal was too hot for his fingers. He set it down on the stove next to the now unnecessary pan.

"You... How?" Cohen's brain was refusing to process, looking for an escape, an out. "You faked that somehow, like a magic trick."

"Not a trick," said Niall. "Magic."

Cohen turned back to Niall, laughter bubbling up as he leaned back on the oven handle to support himself. "This is insane; you're tricking me! It's not funny either," he added seriously, remembering Niall's earlier assertion about the murderer. He shook his head slowly. "Why are you doing this to me?"

"I'm sorry," said Niall, and it looked like he meant it. "I tried not to get you involved. I shouldn't have picked you up yesterday."

"Why did you?" asked Cohen, wondering now if Niall had just been messing with him the whole time.

"Because you needed help," said Niall. "Cohen, please let me put those protections up. I promise I'll explain everything."

"Okay," said Cohen, giving in. "I mean, whatever, they're just dead plants."

"Eat your beans," Niall ordered him. Cohen grabbed his fork and followed Niall out into the foyer.

Niall hung a string on every door and window in the house, and as he did so, he explained everything to Cohen. Jacky and the demon, and the strange magical powers, and how they had been kidnapped by the Guild and escaped. Cohen listened, only half believing, but content to let Niall tell his story anyway, while he ate his beans.

"But what *is* the Guild?" he asked as Niall stood on a stool from the kitchen and pinned little straw men above the doorway to the ballroom. "I mean, are they just some big evil company that likes to kidnap magical children?"

"They're not a company," said Niall, jumping down from the stool. "They're an organisation. Don't go in there, by the way; it's not protected." He gestured at the closed door. "And they're not evil, either. Just corrupt. The thing is, they're necessary because they sort of...regulate the magical world. They keep the general population from knowing about magic, and they stop people who know magic from manipulating the people that don't."

"So, they're like an Evil Ministry of Magic," said Cohen, crossing his arms.

"No. Well, yeah, I suppose. That's simplifying it a bit." Niall sighed. "What I'm trying to say is that from a theoretical point of view, they're good. At the lower levels they function well. Most magic practitioners never really interact with them much besides signing their contracts. As long as you sign the contract, you're protected by them. But it also means they own you."

"Do they own you?" asked Cohen, and Niall nodded.

"That's why I have to put up so many wards, and be so careful. I can only use witchcraft, not my actual magic, because they'll be able to track it."

"How?"

Niall fidgeted with one of the pins. "They have my blood. I signed in blood."

Cohen shook his head, trying to jolt himself back to reality. "This is all *insane*," he said. "Look, I don't believe you."

"It's all right." Niall put the pin back into his suitcase and closed it. Then he reached behind his head and pulled a long cord from around his neck. He handed it to Cohen, who took it automatically. A small wooden charm hung from it, carved with smooth notches in the polished wood. "You don't have to believe me," he said, looking down at the charm. "But at the very least, please wear this. It'll go a long way to keeping you safe from him."

"Him," said Cohen, shivering again. "You mean Jacky? If he's killed people, you should turn him into the police. Why is he trying to set you up?"

Niall's face tightened, and he turned away. "Because I'm trying to stop him."

"Stop him from doing what? From coming after me next? From killing more people?" When Niall didn't reply, Cohen continued. "It doesn't matter. If you turn him in, it'll stop him, and clear your name."

"And the Guild will get him back," said Niall, his voice quiet. "You don't know the things they did to him."

Cohen felt queasy. Whether or not Niall was crazy, he seemed to believe the things he was saying. If he had been kept in prison and tortured for five years, well, that was enough to make anyone crazy. And if he was telling the truth...

"And then I'd have to run again," said Niall, turning back to Cohen. "Before they find me too." He reached out a hand, as if to touch Cohen, and then dropped it quickly, reaching for his coat and striding past him. "I shouldn't have told you so much," he said as Cohen followed him out into the foyer. "I'm probably putting you in more danger the more you know. Please, just wear that amulet, and keep those protections up."

"Why are you so worried about me?" asked Cohen, suddenly not wanting Niall to leave him alone. "Is it because you're afraid Jacky wants me out of the way? Because I provided you with an alibi? Am I safe here?"

"You're safer than most people," said Niall. "I told you before; you're protected from anyone doing magic on you. It's one of the things the Guild does; it puts protections on celebrities, famous people, to keep magical people from tampering with them."

"Are you serious?" Cohen felt faint. "I have magical protections on me?"

Niall nodded. "Jacky won't try to attack you with magic because if he does it will alert the Guild. You're very lucky."

"I'm very insane for believing all this," Cohen corrected him.

Niall gave him a long-suffering look. "Just wear the amulet," he said again. "Keep the protections up." He turned to open the door. Cohen wasn't sure if it was because he was afraid or intrigued or something else entirely, but he wanted Niall to stay. He didn't want to *ask* Niall to stay though, so he kept quiet as Niall turned around to shut the door. He gave Cohen a deadly serious look, the lines on his angular face hard, and his eyes glinting in the dim light from the chandelier. "Please be careful," he said, and the door shut with a heavy thud.

Cohen stood in the cold of the foyer, unsure of what had just happened. He had either just entertained a madman, or else had gotten himself involved in something very, very complicated and bad. Or both.

He climbed the staircase in silence, suddenly feeling very grateful for the stupid dried plant protections and amulet. Then he felt guilty. What would his aunt have thought? But he couldn't bring himself to take the amulet off. It was far too comforting.

Niall had done the upstairs while Cohen had finished eating, and Cohen noticed he had strung more plants along the bannister and on the windows in each room. When he at last entered the bedroom, he stopped short, another chill shooting through him to end this very long, cold day.

The white sheet that he'd pulled off the bed earlier and left crumpled up on the floor was no longer there. It was now draped over the large vanity mirror opposite the bed, carefully, so that not even a sliver of tarnished glass showed through.

The wind had picked up, howling and rattling the window as Cohen stood unmoving, staring at the covered mirror for far too long.

Chapter Five

The moon was nearly half full. The pale silver light streamed down from the ceiling in a glinting beam, illuminating the murk of the cavern. Jacky sat in the dirt, his legs splayed and his eyes glazed over, dreaming of vengeance. His hands were clutched tight around the heart, the blood dripping from it as he squeezed. The slow, lazy patter of droplets falling to the damp earth was the only sound. He hadn't known hearts had so much blood in them.

He roused himself, tearing his eyes away from the beam of moonlight, and stood, clutching the heart carefully to his chest. It was time. He'd been putting it off, dreading the pain. But it had to be done before the full moon, and it was waxing fast.

He approached the dais, flinching a little in the moonlight. The place did not seem made for light; it had gone unlit and unknown for so long. When Jacky had found it and rashly removed the stone from the earth like a stopper from a bottle, the sunlight had streamed down into the temple below, and the statues had seemed to flinch from it. Their stone eyes were blind, but they followed him accusingly, even now. He didn't like them. He would destroy them in the end.

But for now, he had other things to attend to. Flies had found their way down into the temple and buzzed around the two decaying hearts. Jacky leaned forward to inspect them, brushing the flies away as he did so. Along the dais were set five clay bowls, carved in ornate detail. Two of the vessels held hearts, the other three empty and waiting. The child's heart was blackening now; the blood had dried and the meat was beginning to rot. Next to it, in the second vessel, sat the father's, new and rank. The flies favoured it. Jacky slid his free hand along the dust of the dais, over the three vessels still waiting. So many left. But now he had one more.

He brushed his hand over the carved words in the dust. Greek. Luckily, Kathleen had known Greek. Her memories were so very useful.

Child. Father. Sage. Lover. Witch.

The dais was not as old as the thing below. The thing below had been caged there, never to escape. The dais had been made by those who feared the worst. Who believed that a time may come when reign over the beast was necessary, no matter how damning the sacrifices required. Useful memories. Kathleen had found the knowledge frightening when she'd first read it. Now she was like Jacky, full of the knowledge that there were far worse things than hell.

But he didn't like thinking he was anything at all like Kathleen. He caressed the last vessel, and the Greek word *witch*. It was for her; he'd decided that first of all. He was so very impatient for that heart. But he only had two weeks until the full moon, and still two hearts to acquire.

He'd found the sage easily enough, and waited until the perfect moment to use it to his advantage. He could only hope it would be enough to get Niall out of the way. Of course Jacky knew better than to think Niall would ever try to stop him. He'd seen Niall's mind. Niall was too weak, too tied up in morality and fear to cause any problems. Getting Niall arrested wasn't about eliminating a threat; it was about making him safe. All Jacky wanted was for him to be safe.

But he couldn't think about that now. All that was important was that he knew this heart was a suitable sacrifice, and it was time.

He held the heart aloft, his body thrumming with dread. He didn't want to do this. It was going to hurt so very, very much. But it could never hurt as much as what they had done to him. He would pretend it was them in pain, not him, that the Guild would finally be punished for what they had done to him and others like him. And he knew they would. It would take his last breath, and perhaps it would damn him to hell, but they would be punished. That he knew.

He took a deep breath and pressed the heart into the vessel. There was no bright light, no sparks or noises or smoke. This wasn't that kind of magic. There was only absence, as if he had never felt pleasure, or love, or seen light. Darkness and pain and hatred, hatred that ran so deep he could not let go of it. He was looking into the very soul of the beast as it drew its power from him, through the heart, and through his pain. *You will be mine*, Jacky told the beast. *I only need two more hearts, and with them, I will command you, and you will do my bidding.*

The beast was close now. It reached out to invade his mind and loomed there, greater than all of his senses. Jacky was utterly insignificant. The beast drew breath, and smoke and fire and death bellowed forth from its glowing centre. Its voice was like a deep echo in an endless chamber. **And I will do your bidding.**

Cohen leaned forward over the steering wheel, his fingers white from their grip on the keys. The engine turned over again and again, the grating noise assaulting his eardrums, but it refused to start. He leaned back against the torn leather of the seat, sighing heavily, and brought his sore fingers to his mouth, automatically, to chew at his ragged thumbnail. Why couldn't anything go right?

He didn't know what he was going to do now. He'd eaten soup for breakfast and spent the morning clearing all the junk out of the kitchen, piled the boxes of trash into the back of the car, and written up a nice grocery list, ready for his trip into town. And now he was stuck with a car that wouldn't start.

Desperate to distract himself from the stinging in his eyes, he jumped out of the car and walked around to the back, where he opened the rusted petrol cap to peer within. He was pretty sure it was empty. It made sense. The house had been locked up tight, but there was nothing to stop someone from coming by and syphoning all the petrol away. It had been so long, it might have just dried up anyway.

He spent several minutes searching the house and grounds for a can of petrol, but came up with nothing. Of course, that would have been far too easy. He thought of calling someone, but the only person whose phone number he had was Myrna's, and he was pretty sure she had better things to do than personally deliver him petrol.

There was nothing else for it, he decided, as he stood there, hands on his hips and glaring at the useless vehicle. He'd just have to go into town and buy some. He tried to remember how long the drive into town had been yesterday morning. Ten minutes, maybe? It couldn't take that much longer to walk.

The gloom had mercifully cleared up overnight, and the sun was shining warm overhead. Cohen had shrugged his coat off in his search for the non-existent petrol can, but he was forced to put it back on when he re-entered the house, the cold stone walls retaining their chill. He thought briefly about bringing his coat with him on his walk, but there was hardly a cloud in the sky, and it wasn't past noon yet. He'd probably just end up carrying it all the way. He trotted up the stairs and traded it for a hoodie instead.

With some effort, he managed to push the bedroom window open and stood, letting some of the fresh air and warmth in. A light breeze kicked up, stirring the strings of dried plants around. Cohen glared at them critically. Niall probably wouldn't want him walking to town, but the memory of Niall's mystical claims and the depression of yesterday was fading quickly, and it was hard to feel too unhappy or frightened on such a beautiful day.

He grabbed his phone and wallet and took the stairs back down two at a time, whistling as he went. The walk would be a good time to think about the plot of his next book, he decided. He'd start writing it tonight. Or possibly tomorrow morning. But definitely one or the other.

Unfortunately, he didn't end up thinking about his fantasy world on the walk at all, but rather the very strange and potentially more real fantasy world he seemed to have ended up in instead. Niall had definitely made those beans explode last night. Cohen had scraped the last of the evidence off the floor this morning. Could it really be possible that magic was real? The thought made his head spin.

It was also incredibly frightening. If—and he was only allowing the consideration hypothetically—if magic really did exist, and there were people who could use it, that meant he was very, very unsafe. The police would be basically useless against someone who could change their appearance at will, open locks with magic, even control other people. He supposed that was where, according to Niall, the Guild came in. But if Niall was telling the truth, and the Guild had done such horrible things to him and Jacky... Cohen couldn't fathom the idea of such an unfair reality existing. He didn't want to think that the entire world might be under the control of an organisation that could do such terrible things.

But, he thought, kicking at the dirt on the side of the road as he walked, he didn't want to shy away from it either. He could easily pass it off as nonsense. It would be much easier to pretend that he'd never heard about any of it. But what good would that do? Wouldn't that be an act of compliance? Wouldn't that make him just as bad as them?

He shook his head violently. He had to stop thinking like this. He didn't know anything for sure, and the feeling of powerlessness the whole concept gave him was sickening. But what could he do? If Niall was telling the truth, and Jacky had killed people, didn't he have a responsibility to turn Jacky in to the Guild? What was the right thing to do?

It doesn't matter, he told himself firmly. *You don't even know how to contact the Guild, if it even exists, and anyway, Niall's got it under control. Stop thinking about it!* But did Niall have it under control? How did he plan to stop Jacky? Cohen replayed the conversation over again in his mind, trying to remember if Niall had said anything specific about his plan to stop Jacky from killing again. He hadn't told Cohen anything really. Not why Jacky was killing people, or what could be done to stop him. Maybe Niall didn't know.

He pulled out his phone to check the time. He'd been walking for over an hour. His stomach gave a little jolt of panic, and he had to reassure himself that the location of the sun meant he was definitely walking in the right direction. It was just a longer walk than he'd suspected. His feet were beginning to blister, and the sun was hot overhead. He pulled his hoodie off and made a disgusted face when he realised he'd begun to sweat. He tied it around his waist (very fashionable) and picked up his pace a little. He was going to look a right sight when he got into town. Good thing he wasn't looking to make friends or impress anyone.

By the time the little town came into view over a hilltop, Cohen was sweating profusely. His breaths were ragged, and he was certain his feet were blistered. He wanted nothing more than a cold shower and a soft bed, neither of which he was likely to find in town. Oh well, he was only here for petrol. He'd find the nearest petrol station, grab a can, and...lug it all the way back to his house. He sighed heavily. He really hadn't thought this through very well.

Witton was really a tiny town. From his vantage on the hilltop, Cohen could see the single main street that cut directly through the town, with only a few small streets branching off in different directions. It was beautifully quaint though, even from far away. The houses were painted various colours, packed tightly together in town and then becoming more and more sparse as they spread away into the countryside like colourful blocks. The sun was high in the sky now, causing him to shade his eyes and squint, but he thought he could see a petrol station.

He caught his breath, tightened his hoodie around his waist, and began the trek down to town. A solitary car passed him but didn't slow down long enough for Cohen to see the driver. It was only another fifteen minutes or so before the petrol station came into view, luckily on the outskirts of town. It was a flat, metal building with only one pump but attached to what looked like a rather large convenience store. Cohen rushed towards it, grateful for the shade. He didn't see any petrol cans for sale outside, so he pulled the glass door open and stepped inside.

A bell jingled as the door shut behind him, and Cohen looked around at the dimly lit shop. He felt chilled, and realised that he had been sweating. He quickly untied his hoodie and pulled it on, feeling slightly gross.

"Cohen?" said a familiar voice, and Cohen blanched. Niall was emerging from behind the counter, a concerned look on his face. "What are you doing here?"

"Oh," said Cohen, feeling his face heat up with sparks of embarrassment. "You would work here."

"Why, do I suit it?" asked Niall, looking amused, until his face became serious suddenly. "You look exhausted. Did you walk here?"

"I needed petrol. I thought I'd just walk to town and surely I wouldn't meet anyone I know between home and the petrol station—"

Niall walked towards him, looking concerned. "Cohen, do you remember last night when I told you to be careful?"

"My car wouldn't start. What was I supposed to do?" asked Cohen, exasperated. "Anyway, it's the middle of the day, and there was no one around."

"You—" Niall crossed his arms, his face a mixture of annoyance and concern. He looked as handsome as always, although perhaps a little wan. "You walked all the way here, to get petrol," he confirmed. "And you look as if the walk's nearly killed you. What were you going to do after you got the petrol?"

"Well, I was going to rest a bit first," said Cohen, unsure of why he was bothering to defend his sanity when he wasn't sure of it himself. "I dunno."

"Did you wear the charm I gave you, at least?" asked Niall as another customer entered the shop, and he looked relieved when Cohen pulled out the pendant from the long string around his neck. "That's good."

The customer gave Niall a sharp, unfriendly look and strode up to the counter. Niall glanced at Cohen with a long-suffering expression and hurried after the customer.

Cohen drifted over to a rack of crisps near the counter to observe the transaction. The customer was a middle-aged man dressed in dirty, unkempt clothes, and Cohen couldn't tell if he was just a rude person or if he was being particularly short with Niall. He barely spoke to Niall as he grabbed the debit machine from him in a distinctly unfriendly manner and shoved his card in. Niall glanced at Cohen, and the man turned and seemed to notice Cohen for the first time.

"Who are you?" he barked.

Cohen nearly stepped backwards in surprise. "I—I'm new in town. Cohen Brandwein."

The man pulled his card from the machine and leaned on the counter to look at Cohen. "Oh, you're the one who gave the alibi for *him*, aren't you?" He jerked his head in Niall's direction. "Chief Garda mentioned you, only she said you were a boy."

Cohen gritted his teeth. "I am," he said, and his voice came out much weaker than he wanted it to. His voice was changing, slowly, and he could usually produce quite a deep pitch when he wanted to, but of course he utterly failed this time. "I inherited the Coughton from my aunt."

"The old Jewish witch," confirmed the man. "I know. And," he leered, "I know she only had nieces." He stepped forward, advancing on Cohen. "Listen here, *girl*," he said. "There's been a lot of unusual things going on in this town lately, and we don't take kindly to strangers anyhow, especially not ones who are strange to begin with." He turned to look pointedly at Niall, whose jaw was set in a tight line of anger. "Tell you what: you don't try to stand out, and don't go socialising with people who aren't liked, and you'll keep out of trouble. Otherwise..."

"Excuse me," said Cohen, finding his proper voice at last. "Thank you for the advice, but I'm not here to impress anyone. And furthermore, I'll socialise with who I like."

There was a loud noise of paper ripping, and then Niall cut in. "Here's your receipt," he said, holding out a slip of paper. "I'd like you to leave now."

The man turned slowly to Niall and snatched the receipt from his hand. "I'll be speaking to your manager about this," he said. "We don't need any murder suspects working here anyway." He turned to Cohen and tipped his hat in a way that was not at all polite. "Miss," he said and strode out of the shop.

The doorbell chimed, and Cohen nearly fell back into the rack of crisps. He was furious, his whole body shaking. "Oh my god, what an *arsewipe*."

"I am *so* sorry," said Niall, staring at Cohen over the counter. "It's—he was only so rude because you were talking to me. It's all my fault."

"It's not your fault," said Cohen, reaching over to pick up a pack of crisps. He saw what he had been looking for suddenly, a shelf of petrol cans across the shop, and he made for them. Niall followed him.

"That was incredibly brave, what you said to him," Niall said. Cohen felt himself glowing a little from the praise, the warmth slowly reducing the shivers and clutch of dysphoria.

"Thanks," he said. "I'm used to standing up to people, I suppose." When he glanced up, Niall had a look of unabashed admiration on his face. "Oh, stop it," he admonished, but he couldn't help but feel proud of himself as well. "Why was he so rude to you?"

"Oh." Niall shrugged. "Everyone in town is, really. They all think I'm the murderer."

"But I gave you an alibi; they know it wasn't you!"

"Right," said Niall. "Or they think you're in on it."

"Oh." Cohen looked down at the petrol cans, the weight of that fact sinking in. "Well, whatever. I guess I'm not here to make friends. Is this what I need?" He held up a can.

Niall nodded. "I suppose so; I'd have to see your car to be sure. Tell you what." He chewed on his lip a little. "Just, if you wait around a while I'll be off work, and I can drive you back to your place and see that we get your car working."

"Really?" asked Cohen. "That'd be great. I—you're not going to get in trouble, are you? That man said he was going to call and complain about you."

Niall looked out the glass doors to where the man had driven away. "He won't," he said firmly. "And if he does, my manager doesn't care. He's the only one who would give me a job. Here, I'll get it." He lifted the can and carried it over to the counter for Cohen.

"I can carry it," Cohen protested, but Niall insisted on carting it for him.

"No offence, but you look about ready to expire," he said. "Go to the café or the bookshop and get some rest before I drive you home."

"Will I meet more of the charming locals?" Cohen sighed as he pulled out his wallet to pay, and Niall merely grimaced.

When Cohen stepped back out into the sunlight, the parking lot was once again empty. He lifted a hand to shade his eyes and squinted in the direction of town. Niall had said it would be no problem for him to find the café, but Cohen wasn't sure he believed him. Oh well, he was hungry, and in definite need of a coffee. He thought, amused, that maybe his irritability due to lack of caffeine was what had influenced him to stand up to the rude customer.

He shoved his hands into his pockets and began the walk down the road towards town. Although he'd told himself he didn't really care, he hoped fervently that everyone in town wasn't going to be as rude as that man. Well, Myrna wasn't, at least, so he had one friend. And Niall, he supposed, was his friend too, although that relationship was just...strange. He hoped his apparent feelings for Niall weren't clouding his judgement too much, and also that they weren't horribly noticeable. Obviously Niall had a lot on his plate (including a psycho ex-boyfriend) and wasn't exactly in the market for a new boyfriend.

Cohen had never had a boyfriend before, and he'd never allowed himself to think that he might. Liking women was normal for him; he'd identified as a lesbian and had a string of girlfriends before ever coming out as trans. He'd always known he was bi, really, but he'd also always felt like gay men were unattainable to him, like he was an imposter for even being attracted to them.

He remembered his conversation with Niall though, the first night in Witton, before everything had been turned upside down. Niall had sat close to him, and told Cohen that he wouldn't mind dating a man like Cohen. Of course, that didn't mean anything, and Cohen had to decide whether or not he was interested in dating a guy with such obvious issues, if the option presented itself.

Niall had been right about Cohen not being able to miss the café. It was one of about four establishments as he entered the town centre, and the large weathered sign hanging above proclaimed simply "Café." It had glass windows, but the sunlight was so bright Cohen couldn't really see in. It really did seem to be the only place to acquire a meal since the pub across the street didn't look like it would be open until later in the day.

Full of apprehension as he was, Cohen took a firm grip on the heavy wooden door and pulled it open. It swung open easier than he expected, and Cohen flinched and slipped in awkwardly, hoping he hadn't made too much of a scene. He blinked a couple of times as his eyes adjusted, before managing to identify a staff member, a plump Black woman, who was staring at him from behind the counter.

"Oh!" she said. "Hello."

Cohen managed a tight smile, trying not to fidget. "Hello," he replied.

The woman continued staring at him with a confused expression. "Are you passing through then?" she said. "I don't recognise you."

"Oh, no," said Cohen, his heart sinking. Here it went again. "I'm living here now, in the Coughton. It was my aunt's."

The woman's features rearranged themselves into understanding. "Oh, I see!" she said. "Myrna mentioned you, but—" Her voice faltered. "—I thought Miriam only had nieces?"

Cohen forced his smile to stay in place. "Nope," he said. "My name's Cohen."

If the woman continued to be confused, she didn't show it. "Well, come in," she said, gesturing Cohen forward. "What can I get you? I'm Grace by the way."

As Cohen stepped forward, he became aware that there were several other people sitting in the booths and at the tables around the shop, and all of them were staring at him. Only a few were doing it openly of course, the others glancing at him surreptitiously over coffee and books. Most of them seemed to be middle-aged or over. Cohen tried to ignore them, ordering a coffee and a pastry for lunch.

He paid, collected his food, and went to sit in a booth by the window, all the while feeling eyes on him. He wished he'd brought a book or something, but settled for taking his phone out and connecting to the Wi-Fi. Eventually, when he neglected to do anything interesting, he felt the stares recede, and he settled in to eat his pastry.

The door opened a couple of times as people came and went. A few of them sat down to eat; a few simply left with their coffee. All of them stared at Cohen, but luckily none of them spoke to him. Cohen sat with his head down, flicking through websites on his phone and wondering how he was going to get through the rest of the day. He was feeling quite depressed, and more than a little homesick. He longed for the city where no one knew anyone, and he could walk into a coffee shop without getting stared at like he had two heads. Why had he thought moving to a small town would be a good idea?

The door opened again, and Cohen looked up, against his better judgement. A thrill of relief went through him as he recognised the new arrival. Myrna was pulling off her heavy blue-and-yellow coat and striding up to the counter, greeting Grace with a friendly nod. She turned around to glance out the window and saw Cohen, surprise crossing her features.

"Oh, hello!" she said, leaning on the counter as she passed a bill to Grace. "Did you get your groceries?"

Cohen shook his head, aware that everyone was once again staring at him. "Not yet," he admitted. "I had a problem with my car, so I walked to town."

Myrna tutted. "And I told you to be safe," she chided. She lifted her head, tilting it to the side a little, and glancing around the shop at the impolite eavesdroppers. "Care to have coffee with me outside?" she asked Cohen, who gratefully accepted.

They sat in the sun at one of the little rusted tables, and Myrna sipped her coffee, staring at Cohen over her mug with sharp green eyes. "How are you, then?" she asked. "Feeling all right after yesterday?"

Cohen shrugged. "Yeah, I suppose. I, um." For a moment, he wanted to tell her about Niall coming to visit him, and what he'd said about Jacky, but something stopped him. He suddenly felt very cliché. Wasn't this what people in fantasy novels always did after finding out about magical conspiracies? Failed to tell the authorities. But what was he supposed to tell Myrna? It sounded mad even thinking it in his head.

"You..." prompted Myrna, jolting him back into reality. "You said you walked here? Why didn't you call me? I could have picked you up, or put you in contact with a repairman."

"I didn't think of that," admitted Cohen. "I mean, I thought of calling you, but I figured you'd be working."

"Well, I was," said Myrna. "We've been scouring Sandy's apartment for evidence all morning. I found a day-planner confirming that she scheduled picking you up at six, so that clears Niall's name a little further."

"Well that's good," sighed Cohen. "Maybe you can inform the locals of that as well, and they'll get off his back."

"Have you seen him since?" asked Myrna, looking concerned.

"He was at the station where I went to get petrol. There was a man there." Cohen felt his face scrunching, his anger flaring up at the memory. "He was really rude to Niall, and to me. I guess he doesn't believe that Niall's not the murderer, and he thinks I'm in on it."

Myrna gave a frustrated sigh. "I'm sorry about that," she said. "What did he look like?"

"Just an older man," said Cohen. "Sort of a grey face, dirty hat."

"Mm," Myrna nodded. "That's Clinton Soch. It was his niece that was murdered last month."

"Oh." Cohen immediately felt sick. "That—I didn't know."

"It doesn't excuse him being rude to you, of course," said Myrna, shaking her head. "I wish you'd come here before all this. The locals..." She glanced at the window. "They weren't always like this. It used to be a nice tourist town, beautiful views, honeymoon destination." She chuckled. "There are some ancient stone circles in the countryside that 'rival Stonehenge' according to the tourist guide, right on the way to your house, to the west. But—" She sighed again. "You know how it is; everyone is frightened now. And I feel—" She broke off, staring guiltily at Cohen. "I'm sorry, I don't mean to bore you with all this."

"Oh, you don't!" Cohen reassured her. "Really, I don't mind, I'm a good listener. It's part of being a writer."

"Is that right?" Myrna laughed. "My daughter is dying to meet you, you know. Would you like to come over tonight?"

Niall was driving him home tonight. Cohen immediately felt guilty that he rated that prospective visit higher than dinner with Myrna. "Ah, well I've got to get my car fixed," he explained. "I mean hopefully it just needs petrol. But how about tomorrow night?"

Myrna smiled, the harsh lines of her face becoming softer with it. "I'll cook dinner for seven o'clock," she said, pulling out her notebook to write her address down. "You shouldn't have too much trouble finding it," she assured him, and Cohen thought she was probably right.

★

Myrna left shortly after that, and Cohen sat finishing his coffee and feeling guilty. He really ought to have told her about Niall. She'd been kind to Cohen and was obviously competent, and he was purposely keeping her out of the loop. But then again, he would feel just as guilty, if not more so, revealing to Myrna what Niall had obviously told him in the strictest of confidence. He simply didn't know enough to gauge what the right thing to do was. Niall hadn't really told him anything, and it was still possible that he was completely crazy, in which case telling Myrna would definitely be the best thing to do.

He should press Niall for more information tonight. Then he could decide on the best course of action. He'd make him do something else magical to prove it was real.

Cohen threw away his rubbish and folded his hoodie over his arm. Myrna had told him there was shopping a short walk north, so he headed off in that direction. He felt strangely let down. His entire childhood he'd wished magic was real, dreamed that he'd meet someone with magical powers, or develop some himself. But his eleventh birthday had come and gone with no Hogwarts letter in sight, and he'd come to realise it was probably for the best. Magic was all fine and good for a child, but in the real world, actions had consequences, and magic definitely wasn't synonymous with wonder. What a child might use as a toy, an adult would use as a weapon.

He hated the disillusionment. It made his skin crawl. But he couldn't decide which option was worse: that Niall was crazy, or that magic (in all of its grim, fatal glory) was real. The former was the easy way out, but the latter was strangely tempting. Especially because of Niall. Cohen didn't want him to be crazy. And part of him hoped that beyond all the horror and grim reality, a spark of that wonder still lay.

People are dead, he reminded himself sternly. *Magic or not, it's a serious situation.*

And there he was back to feeling guilty about not telling Myrna everything he knew. He was going around in circles and getting nowhere. He wouldn't get anywhere until he talked to Niall tonight. That was, if Niall was even interested in talking to him.

He decided to get a vegetarian option for dinner just in case. The shop was easy to find and nice enough, in a quaint, dusty sort of way. Cohen thought that Niall's petrol station might have had almost as good a selection. He wondered if the shop had better business now that Niall was a suspected murderer.

The only other person in the place was the clerk, an old man with a bald head and little round glasses. He was sitting behind the wooden counter reading a newspaper, and completely ignored Cohen when he entered except to give him a quick, withering glance and return to his newspaper.

"Hello!" said Cohen in his most chipper voice, because he was getting tired of being stared at over the top of newspapers, but the man continued to ignore him.

Well, at least he hadn't asked Cohen where he was staying.

By the time he'd gotten his entire order together, it was nearly five o'clock. The sun was hanging low in the sky, and warm light was filtering through the small, dusty windows of the shop. Cohen squinted as he loaded his shopping onto the counter and waited while the clerk rang them through the ancient register. The price was outrageous, of course, but his mother had warned him that groceries would be more expensive out of town.

He chose paper bags, intending to recycle them and impress Niall, and then loaded them all into his arms and hobbled to the door. The clerk followed him, all the time not saying a word, and watched him leave, slamming the door shut behind Cohen. Cohen glanced at the hours printed on the window, and noted with a sinking feeling that the shop closed at five. That meant not only had he kept the man at his shop past closing, but he was going to be late meeting Niall.

He clutched the bags to his chest in a panic and began to race back down the street to the petrol station. By the time he arrived, he was sweating again, the bags were crumpled against him, and his arms were stiff from holding them. He didn't see Niall's truck right away, and for a moment he worried that Niall had left without him, until he turned the corner and saw the blue truck parked behind the station. Niall was leaning against the door in the sunlight, and he smiled when he saw Cohen and straightened up to wave. He'd unbuttoned the front of his uniform a little, and the flash of muscled torso that Cohen caught nearly caused him to drop all of his bags.

"Are you okay?" Niall asked, lunging forward to help Cohen. "I could have brought you to the shop."

"It's fine," gasped Cohen. "I should have gotten bags with handles; I was just trying to be economical."

Niall smiled, and Cohen noticed that his eyes crinkled at the corners when he did so. He took the bags from Cohen, grinning, and loaded them in behind the seats. "Get in," he said, jerking his head at the passenger seat, and Cohen complied, glancing back to see that Niall had already loaded up the petrol and that useless bag of crisps he'd bought.

"Thank you," Cohen said as Niall slammed the back door shut and jumped into the driver's seat. "You've done so much for me."

Niall laughed again. He started the ignition and leaned back to reverse out of the lot. Cohen tried not to look at the sliver of muscles showing down the front of Niall's unbuttoned shirt as he reached over to look back, but it was difficult. His face felt hot, and not just from the exertion. "Well, I owe you," said Niall as they pulled onto the highway. "I'd be in jail if it weren't for you."

"I guess," said Cohen. Niall drove them out onto the road, and the bushes and fences began to whip by. Niall rolled down the window, and the warm air blustered in. Cohen could feel it stirring his hair into wild curls. He reached up, desperately trying to settle it, but the effort was futile. Niall noticed and leaned forward to roll the window up.

"Sorry," he said. "I'm always too hot."

"It's okay." Cohen reached up to pull down the visor, but found that the mirror there had been completely obscured with masking tape.

"Don't," said Niall softly as Cohen reached up to touch the peeling swaths of tape.

Cohen glanced at him. "You don't like mirrors. Bad luck?"

Niall shook his head. He was smiling, but the crinkle at the corners of his eyes was notably absent. He stared at the road, but didn't say anything.

The trip back to the Coughton was over in a ridiculously short time considering how long Cohen had walked. Niall inspected Cohen's car for a few moments and confirmed that the petrol had indeed evaporated, and Cohen needed a new cap for his tank to avoid it happening again. He poured the new gas into the tank and checked to make sure the car started while Cohen took the groceries into the kitchen.

"You're all set," he said, tossing the keys back to Cohen. "Don't fill the whole thing up until you can get to the shop to get that replaced, or it'll happen again in this heat."

"Okay," Cohen said, nodding, and then blurted, "Would you like to stay for dinner?"

Niall looked surprised. "I... Cohen, I shouldn't."

"Why not?" Cohen desperately wanted him to stay. He needed to find out more about what was going on, and also he just desperately wanted Niall to stay. "I mean, you said I'm in danger. Isn't it sort of safer if you stay?"

"Well, I guess, but—" Niall looked confused. "I assumed you'd want to stay out of it."

"Well." Cohen gulped. "You thought wrong. I want to know what's going on. And I want to help if I can. And—" He bit his lip and pressed on. "—I'd like you to stay for dinner. In fact, you have to stay for dinner, because if you don't tell me what's going on properly, I'm going to go to Myrna and tell her everything you told me last night."

Niall raised his eyebrows. "Are you blackmailing me?"

"No!" said Cohen, even though that was what it sounded like. "It's just that I can't sit by and let bad things happen without doing something about it. I have to know what's going on, so I can make the right decision. You understand, right?" He hoped Niall did because he didn't want to make Niall hate him.

But Niall didn't look angry. "I understand," he said. "All right, I'll stay for dinner. And I'll try to explain things better. But listen, Cohen, if you get involved in this, it could be really dangerous."

"I know that," said Cohen, and his heart leapt uncomfortably in his chest. "Life's dangerous. But listen, I bought stuff for a vegetarian dinner, so you'd better stay."

Niall laughed, and Cohen was pleased to see the corners of his eyes crinkle again. "All right, I'll stay."

Chapter Six

Niall grabbed a change of clothes from the back of his truck and went upstairs to change in the bathroom while Cohen set about making a pot of mushroom soup. It was freezing in the house. The cold stone walls seemed impervious to the heat outside, and Cohen could almost feel the cold radiating through the carpet below him as he made his way to the kitchen. He shivered and zipped his hoodie up, then turned on the oven again for warmth as he stirred the soup.

Niall appeared a few minutes later wearing a pair of jeans and a T-shirt, the unbuttoned uniform shirt sadly nowhere in sight. "Cooking the old-fashioned way, I see," he joked.

"Yeah, well I didn't really feel like cleaning up chunks of mushroom from all over the kitchen," replied Cohen. "Does magical cooking require explosions?"

"Only if I'm doing it, apparently. Dishes?"

"They're all dusty; you'll have to wash them. Luckily I grabbed soap." Cohen ducked down to pull the bottle of dishwashing liquid from one of the bags.

"Cheers," said Niall, taking the soap from Cohen, and they set about getting ready for dinner. It felt just like dinners at home with his family. He wondered what Niall's family was like.

"Thanks for staying for dinner," he said after a while. Not to fill the silence—it wasn't the uncomfortable sort—but because he really did enjoy having Niall there.

"Thanks for having me," Niall replied simply, and Cohen felt a tinge of frustration. This was a little too polite and cold, the conversation stiff and rehearsed. He wanted more.

"It's lonely here," he admitted. "I thought it would be nice to be alone for once, but it's a bit *too* much, you know?"

"You're close to your family?" Niall asked. He was washing all of Cohen's dishes, setting them to dry on a dish towel with quick, sure movements.

"My sister and I were homeschooled," said Cohen. "And my dad works from home. We live in a pretty small flat, so yeah, we're always on top of each other."

"I'd be scared of this big old house if I were you," said Niall, glancing around. "I mean, not me; I grew up in an old house, but they're different from flats."

"I like it," said Cohen. "It feels more real, I guess."

"You're a romantic," said Niall with a small smile.

"I'm a writer," agreed Cohen.

"You're a fantasy writer, specifically," agreed Niall. "All about nostalgia and escapism, right?"

"Not necessarily," said Cohen. "But I guess my books were. I kind of had this longing for a world where things were simpler and more complex at the same time." Niall gave him a questioning look, so he continued. "I mean, we live in a world where daily life is boring and morality is complex."

"You want the opposite?"

"I did," said Cohen. "But I guess it's stupid to think that just because daily life gets more complex, morality will get easier."

"Morality always gets more complex." Niall sighed, drying bowls now and setting them on the table. He sat and leaned forward on his arms. "The more confused I get, the more simple I want my life to be. What do you do when faced with a moral quandary?" He looked up at Cohen, who realised that he was asking as a legitimate enquiry.

"You try to make the best decision?" Cohen suggested as he balanced the pot of hot soup to the table and put it down on top of one of the oven mitts. "You pray about it?"

"Do you?" Niall asked. "Pray?"

Cohen sat, feeling queasy. Well, he'd wanted a deeper discussion and gotten it. "Not really. I used to. My family is really secular, but I sort of picked up on it as a kid. I thought it could help me with all the bad things I was feeling."

"Did it?" Niall was ignoring the soup, looking at Cohen instead.

"I thought so," sighed Cohen. "You know how a lot of people come out as kids? But I managed to repress it for years, so I don't know," he concluded. "I think praying just helps you to go through with the things you've already decided to do."

"I can't decide what to do," said Niall, reaching for the soup at last. "So that doesn't really help."

"I'm sorry," said Cohen. "What are you trying to decide on?"

Niall smiled sadly. "It's not really a topic for dinner conversation."

"Tell me later, then," said Cohen and Niall agreed.

After dinner, they headed upstairs to Cohen's bedroom to take advantage of the space heater. Niall, however, stopped Cohen when he went to start it up, and instead knelt by the fireplace. There was no wood, and Cohen had no idea what he was doing, until Niall started to mumble under his breath and placed his hands on the hearth. Suddenly a purple light flashed and sparkling flames crept up, bringing with them heat and a warm, flickering light.

"Oh my god," breathed Cohen, bending down to survey the fire, which seemed to be burning from nothing but darkness. "Oh my god, you— Niall, this is—" This was so much more real than the exploding can of beans. This fire was real and warm and so obviously magical that it made his head spin.

"Magic," said Niall, a little smugly. "I told you."

"But—I—" Cohen backed away from the fireplace, staring from Niall to the fireplace and then back to Niall. "Was that really powerful magic? Won't they be able to track you?"

"They won't. It was just minor witchcraft," said Niall. "People do it all the time; they don't bother to pick up on it. And anyway, I've got these wards up, remember? They can't see inside."

Cohen stared at the fire for a little longer. "I need to sit down," he announced at last and did so on the bed. Niall sat next to him.

"I learned all this stuff from inside Kathleen's head," he explained softly. "Jacky and I—we were just kids when they took us. We wouldn't have been able to survive on the outside without her. She knows so much."

"When you..." Cohen shivered. Magic was real. And everything Niall had told him was real. "You," he whispered, turning to look at Niall's face in the firelight. "You were locked up, for *years*. How are you okay? How are you not *s-so* angry?" His voice shook with the injustice of it. He wanted to grab Niall and hold him tight, save him somehow, even though it had already been done.

"I—" Niall looked stricken for a moment. "I don't know. I am. I think. It's so hard to feel anything. I think I'm fine, and then I have such bad dreams. Sometimes I think it's not real. That I'm still in there; they're just tricking me." His eyes darted to the mirror on Cohen's dresser. Cohen had removed the sheet on it, and Niall was staring at it with fear in his eyes.

Cohen jumped up, grabbed the sheet from the floor, and tossed it over the mirror so that it was completely covered. That seemed to relax Niall, and he slumped. "Thank you," he breathed. "I'm sorry, it's just...mirrors. They used to watch us through two-way mirrors." He looked away from Cohen, the lines of his cheeks clenched in frustration. "I know it's not logical. I just can't help but feel like someone's always watching me."

Cohen walked towards Niall tentatively. "I'm sorry for asking you about it," he said. "I didn't mean to dredge up bad memories."

"It's okay," said Niall, and he stared at the mirror for a few more minutes before glancing at Cohen. "You're shivering," he said, looking concerned.

"Oh." Cohen's arms crept around him. "Yeah, it's just cold." That wasn't the real reason he was shaking, of course, but he didn't want Niall to know how angry and upset he was.

"You might as well get under the blankets," said Niall, gesturing to the bed. "If you want I can hold you. I mean to warm you up. I'm always warm." He looked embarrassed, but he was still looking at Cohen, the embarrassment in his eyes second fiddle to sincerity.

Cohen shivered again, but this time at the thought of Niall touching him. Not even in a sexual way, just in the desperate way he'd wanted to hold him and take his pain away. "Okay, yeah," he said, and his lips trembled a little. He really was cold. "Okay," he said again and then hurried to take his shoes off and scramble under the covers.

Niall followed him, holding the blanket up as they both got under the heavy comforter, fully clothed. Cohen set up the pillows, and then Niall put his arm up around Cohen's shoulder, and Cohen snuggled into him. He *was* warm, like a thrumming centre of heat, and his body through his thin T-shirt felt hard and angular and *so* comfortable. "Oh, god," he whispered. "That is so much better."

Niall wasn't saying anything, but his breathing was hard and Cohen could feel his heart beating in his chest.

"Are you okay?" he asked, looking up at Niall, who glanced down at him.

"God, yeah," he said. "I'm sorry, it's just been so long since I touched someone."

Cohen frowned and snuggled closer. "But didn't you...with Jacky?"

"Not after we escaped," said Niall, his body stiffening again with the memory. "He didn't like to be touched anymore, and I wasn't sure if I wanted to touch him anyway. I thought he'd get better. I thought we could both get better."

"What happened?" asked Cohen. "You didn't tell me what you did after you escaped."

Niall took a deep breath and let it out slowly. "We left London. Went to Russia, actually. Kathleen speaks Russian so we both can too. *Ruskij*. I got a job there, and we rented a place. I was careful about everything, and so was Jacky. I thought, I really thought he'd start to get better."

"But he didn't?" mumbled Cohen, wishing he weren't making Niall talk about this, but suspecting that Niall wanted to talk about it anyway.

"You know how I'm not really angry?" Niall shifted, and Cohen straightened up so that he could look at Niall. "I guess I had to give up on anger because otherwise it would drive me mad. I think it drove Jacky a little mad. Or maybe he was mad already, and this just gave him something to aim for. He became obsessed with destroying the Guild, bringing it down. I agreed that maybe there was something we could do to stop them taking advantage of people, but nothing violent."

"Violent," repeated Cohen. "What does he want to do to them?"

"I don't know," sighed Niall. "I didn't like looking into his mind too much. I just know he has so much anger there that he doesn't care about people dying, or even about himself dying."

"But why is he here?" Cohen pressed. "Why is he killing people here? One of his victims was a little girl; she can't have had anything to do with the Guild."

"He's using them as sacrifices," said Niall. "There used to be Druids here, in this part of Ireland. They found a pit with something in it, something that had been locked away a long time ago, to keep it from destroying the world. Or that's what the legend says anyway."

"A Titan?" whispered Cohen. "Like when Zeus locked away the Titans? That kind of thing actually *happened*?"

"I don't know," said Niall. "Probably something *like* that anyway. So the Druids set up a way to free the Titan and control it, if the need ever arose."

"That's completely *stupid*," gasped Cohen. "That's more stupid than summoning a demon! No offence."

"Summoning a demon *was* the stupidest thing we've ever done," agreed Niall. "And now he's going to go and do something even more stupid."

"You *have* to stop him," said Cohen, nearly jumping out of the bed with urgency. "Niall, you *can't* let him do that."

"What am I supposed to do?" asked Niall. "Turn him in to the Guild? I might as well turn us both in. He'd rather die than go back to them, and so would I. Should I kill him? Or let the Guild do that, slowly?" He was angry, his body stiff, no longer touching Cohen.

"You can't just let him get away with what he's doing, though! He's killing people! It'd be the lesser of two evils."

"Right," agreed Niall. "Fine, you're right—he needs to die. You've made that decision, so why don't you carry it out?"

A cold shiver passed through Cohen. He swallowed, a lump hard in his throat. "I—I couldn't," he whispered.

"I know," said Niall, his voice cracking. "I couldn't either. And because of that, I'm just sitting here letting him kill people, but what am I supposed to do?"

"I don't know," said Cohen, finally recognising the moral quandary that Niall was in. "You could try to talk to him again to stop him?"

"He's hell-bent on it," said Niall. He wrapped his arms around himself and sunk into the bed. "I suppose I could try again."

"No." Cohen reached toward Niall, wanting to touch him again, wanting to comfort him, but feeling like his comfort was utterly useless. "I'm so sorry. I didn't mean to judge you like that."

To Cohen's surprise, Niall reached forward and touched his hand, slipping his strong fingers between Cohen's soft, shorter ones. Then he reached forward with his other hand and touched it to Cohen's face. Cohen gasped, the touch shocking. He felt like his heart was going to burst. All at once, he wanted to flinch away and cry and then reach forward and kiss Niall so hard that he forgot about everything else.

Niall's fingers were clenching Cohen's hand tightly, while the fingers of his other hand made their way to the back of Cohen's neck to tangle in his hair. He seemed to realise what he was doing and tried to pull away, but Cohen kept his hand there, holding tight.

"You shouldn't get involved in this," Niall said firmly, still trying to tug his hand away. "You shouldn't get involved with me."

"I wish I hadn't," admitted Cohen. "But now I have, and I can't just go back and pretend this never happened. I'm involved now. I want to help."

"You can't help," said Niall.

"But I can try." Cohen reached out and began to copy Niall's actions, moving his hand over Niall's cheek, the skin soft but peppered with sharp stubble, and then back over Niall's strong jaw and into the soft warmth at the nape of his neck. "I don't know why I'm feeling this way. I promise it's not because you're dangerous or exciting or anything like that. I wish we were both completely normal."

He realised the double meaning to that as soon as he said it and became aware of his body once again, all the ways it was wrong—for himself and for Niall. He could feel the binder pressing against his chest, and the way he should be reacting to Niall's smell and his warmth but wasn't.

"You feel normal to me," said Niall, so soft it was almost a whisper, but with the strength of his voice behind it. "You feel like..." He seemed lost for words, his mouth open. As if he was waiting for what he wanted to say to come, but he had forgotten, or whatever it was didn't exist, hadn't up until this moment.

Cohen kissed him.

He'd never felt anyone react to a kiss the way Niall did. It was as if his entire body caught fire, like a roaring beast of desperation had burst out of him. He pressed forward, engulfing Cohen with his mouth, his warmth almost overbearing but irresistible. Their mouths opened and Niall's tongue slipped in, teasing the roof of Cohen's mouth until he moaned from the shivers of pleasure.

Niall's hands were on Cohen, like hard clamps digging into the soft flesh of Cohen's waist, pulling him closer. He leaned over Cohen, pressing his thigh between Cohen's legs, and Cohen clung to Niall desperately, hopeless and helpless in the face of Niall's desperation.

He could hardly breathe, but air seemed less important than the feel of Niall's wet tongue and lips against his mouth. Cohen dug his fingers into the muscle of Niall's back, pulling him closer. It was as if Niall wanted to devour him, and Cohen wanted to be devoured; he had never felt such heat, never wanted so badly. There was a fire between his legs, burning him up, threatening to tear him in two.

He squirmed a little and moaned Niall's name, and Niall seemed to come to his senses. "Oh my god," he gasped and threw himself off Cohen, backing up from him with a look of panic in his eyes. "Oh my god, Cohen, I'm so sorry!"

"Uh," gasped Cohen, because he seemed to be incapable of making any other noises. He shoved himself up from where he had been lying flat on his back and pressed his legs together. His groin was on fire, a searing, throbbing slash like he'd just had his dick cut off a second ago. It wasn't an altogether unpleasant feeling, but he could have gone without the mental analogy. "Feeling a little deprived?" he asked Niall, who looked like he was about to explode with embarrassment.

"I honestly don't know what came over me," he said through his hands. "That sounds horrible and cliché, but it's true."

"I'm just that sexy," quipped Cohen, and Niall lowered his hands, his gaze hot on Cohen.

"You are," he said. Cohen wanted to make a token protest, but Niall was obviously telling the truth, and who was he to argue? "Was that okay?"

"More than okay," Cohen reassured him. "But I... I should stop you before we go any further, because I—" He sighed. "I can't do a lot of things that, you know, *normal—* cis," he corrected himself, "people can do."

Niall leaned forward to draw Cohen back into his arms, pulling the blanket up over them. "It's okay," he said. "I'm okay with doing whatever you wanna do."

"I-I've only been with girls before," Cohen blurted out.

"But you like guys, right?" asked Niall, looking concerned. "Because you seemed..."

Cohen laughed. "I like guys, but I worry that guys won't like me. See, I don't...because of how my body is, I can't..." Cohen sighed with frustration at the thought. "I can't really handle being touched. It wasn't a problem with girls because I was always, you know, the active partner."

"Ah, I see." Niall went in for another kiss, this one soft and controlled. "You can be the active partner with me too."

Cohen felt his heart leap into his throat with excitement at the thought. "But..." He frowned. "That defies all yaoi stereotypes."

"You're right; I hadn't thought of that," said Niall, looking for all the world like he was wrestling with a grave issue. Cohen gave a snort of laughter, and Niall's face broke into a wide, happy grin.

"God, Cohen, you make me laugh," he said, as if Cohen had given him the greatest gift imaginable, and he pulled Cohen tight against him in a crushing hug. Cohen hugged him back, loving the feel of him, loving the thought that he had somehow managed to at least distract Niall from his sadness. He wasn't useless after all.

Niall tilted his head down to kiss Cohen once again, and the hug quickly morphed into something much less innocent. Niall's hands were careful to stay away from Cohen's chest or groin, but Cohen loved the feel of them on his back and waist. He began to run his hands over Niall's back, and then, when Niall didn't protest, his sides. God, Niall had muscle. Real, strong, firm muscles like Cohen had never felt before. His curiosity almost as strong as his desire, he lifted the bottom of Niall's shirt and ran a finger along his hip.

Niall gasped into Cohen's mouth and moaned as Cohen's hands roamed higher. Niall's muscles felt hard and smooth under his skin. Cohen wondered what it would be like to have such a strong body. He wondered if Niall didn't prefer to touch people that felt like him, all hard angles and tight muscles. What did Cohen feel like to Niall?

Niall broke away from Cohen for a moment, and Cohen realised that he was pulling his T-shirt off over his head. He was distracted from his doubts for the moment, looking at Niall's body. He was long and lean, hardly an ounce of fat on him. His nipples were small and pert, his torso long and defined, a perfect six-pack joining in jutting hips to point to the trail of brown hair that led down below the waistline of his pants.

Cohen suddenly felt overdressed in his hoodie. It was warm enough in here now, with the magical fire and all the burning desire. He stripped to his T-shirt and reached forward to touch Niall again, moving his hands to the gap between Niall's hips and the fabric of his jeans.

"Can I?" he asked, tugging at the button on Niall's jeans, and Niall nodded. For a moment, Cohen thought he was really going to go through with it.

Then the dysphoria that he had been trying so very hard to suppress rose to the surface. "No, Niall, I'm so sorry. I can't." He fell back, pressing his hands to his face. Too much...it was too much.

"Cohen?" Niall was on his knees in a minute, leaning towards Cohen in concern. "What is it?"

"I can't," said Cohen. The back of his throat was burning. He felt sick to his stomach. "I can't touch you, Niall, I'm sorry, I can't."

"It's all right," Niall reassured him. "It's all right really, but why?"

"I've never touched a man," Cohen explained through the thickness in his throat and the creeping wrongness that was seeping through his body. "It's—it's what I'm supposed to look like, to *feel* like, but I don't know how it feels, so it's okay."

"I..." Niall looked worried. "I'm sorry, Cohen. I don't understand."

"It's just—" Cohen took a deep breath and tried desperately to form his feelings into words. "I'm afraid if I touch you, if I know how a man feels, then I'll know what I'm supposed to feel like. I'm afraid it will make my dysphoria worse, and I don't know if I could handle that."

"I'm sorry." Niall had that stricken look on his face again. "Cohen, I'm sorry. I didn't know."

"It's not your fault," sighed Cohen. "I didn't tell you. I didn't even realise it really until right now. I-I mean, I thought it would just happen and it would be fine, but..." He hated himself so much sometimes. He was such a coward, letting his dysphoria get in the way of everything just because he couldn't handle a little sickness.

"We'll stop." Niall was reaching for his shirt, pulling it over his head. "I do understand, Cohen. It's okay. I'll even leave if you want."

"I don't want you to leave," said Cohen derisively. It was selfish to want Niall to stay, but he didn't care. "I want you to stay anyway, even though I don't have anything to give you."

Niall put his hands on Cohen's shoulders and pulled him into another tight hug. "I'll be here as long as you'll let me," he said. "What would you like? Would you like me to sleep in the spare bedroom? Is it...is it okay if I sleep here?"

"Would you?" asked Cohen, looking up at him. It was as if the dark, cold house was closing in on him, and the last thing he wanted right now was to be alone.

"I'd love to," said Niall. "We can sleep together. Like actually sleep."

"I have to sleep with my binder off," realised Cohen, with another icy spurt of dysphoria. It was creeping through him steadily now, taking over all his reserves of happiness and settling in like a bout of winter depression.

"If that's fine with you, it's fine with me," said Niall.

Cohen went to the bathroom alone to get ready for bed. He pulled off his shirt and binder and changed into his baggiest night shirt. Then he clutched his arms across himself, aware that no matter how baggy his top was, his chest was obvious. Niall had said he didn't care. Now Cohen got to find out if that was true or not. Not that it mattered anymore if Niall was attracted to him since they wouldn't be having sex.

Niall had dimmed the fire and was sitting on the bed in only his boxers and T-shirt. He was so goddamned perfect. Cohen had never had bad self-esteem. He'd always been defensive of his chubby body, and relied on the fact that his personality was attractive enough to push past any conventionally unattractive aspects of his appearance. Now, standing in his bedroom across from a man who was perfectly beautiful on the outside, but horribly scarred on the inside, he felt kind of lucky.

"I'm coming to bed," he announced, and Niall nodded, lifting up the blankets so they could both crawl underneath. Cohen turned away from Niall, who curled up behind him and slid a tentative hand around Cohen's stomach, careful not to roam too high or too low.

"I'm sorry," murmured Niall, "if I made it worse, somehow."

Cohen curled up a little tighter and lowered his head, speaking so quietly he wasn't sure if Niall could hear him. "It's always bad. I have my shot tomorrow, so I should feel better then."

Niall was quiet for a long time. Finally, he asked, sounding half-asleep. "What does it feel like?"

"The shot?"

"The dysphoria."

Cohen felt his mouth twitch. *Did they ever tie you up?* He wanted to ask Niall. *Did they give you medication so you couldn't move, or so your body didn't feel like it belonged to you anymore?* "I don't want to talk about what it feels like," he said.

"I'm sorry," said Niall, and they were quiet until Cohen finally fell into a restless sleep.

Chapter Seven

It felt like a nightmare. Like a demon on his chest, suffocating him. Cohen pushed away the blankets, desperately tearing at his shirt, trying to get free, but to no avail. He lay in bed, staring at the darkness above him, listening to the thud of his heartbeat in his ears.

He had to get it off.

Carefully, so as not to wake Niall, he sat up and went to the door. The room seemed strange, the fire blurry and the walls dark. It wasn't his normal room, was it? Where was he?

He felt his way down the hall to the stairway. His hands tangled in the strings of magic on the railing, and he struggled to pull them free. Trapped, suffocating. He pressed his hands to his chest, clawing at it, but the weight remained. *Get free, get free...* But where could he go?

He stumbled down the stairs and into the kitchen, more by feel than by sight. Why was it so dark? And what was he looking for again? There, spread on the counter like dim white spheres, and next to them a clash of silver. Cohen reached for them, sifting through to find the knife.

He reached for the neck of his T-shirt, the strangling, scratchy fabric, and pulled it over his head. He ran his fingers over the scars. Failed attempts. This time he would do it, though. This time he was strong enough. His breathing was erratic; blackness was obscuring his vision. He felt the tip of the knife, pressed it to the skin on his chest. The metal was cool, and the prick was hot as the blood began to flow.

"Cohen!"

Cohen screamed as a blinding light flooded down from above. He dropped the knife and it clanged to the floor. As his eyes adjusted, he could make out the figure of Niall standing in the doorway, and suddenly Cohen was aware that his chest was bare, and his feet were frozen to the cold kitchen floor.

"Cohen, are you all right?" Niall lunged towards him, and Cohen backed away, pressing his arms over his chest. His heart was beating fast and desperate, his skin prickling painfully.

"God, Niall, don't look at me, please." Cohen turned away, bending over the counter behind him, wishing he could curl into nothing. He felt bile at the back of his throat again, and his mouth was full of thick copper. "Just go away." He could feel Niall's footsteps coming closer, and he jerked away desperately. "Niall, please don't look at me!"

Niall's footsteps stopped. "I'm sorry, Cohen. I just need to know that you're all right."

"I'm fine now. I'm awake."

"You were sleepwalking?"

"I do that." Cohen made his way to the sink and spat, trying desperately to clear his mouth. He reached for one of the glasses on the counter and poured himself a drink of metallic-tasting water.

"You're bleeding," said Niall, and Cohen looked down at his bare chest. The cut was just above his left nipple, and a thick trail of dark blood rolled down over the breast tissue and onto his stomach. He wiped at it before it could stain the waistband of his trousers. Niall was looking at his chest, but Cohen couldn't summon up the energy to care anymore.

"I'm fine," Cohen sighed. "It's all right; this used to happen all the time, see?"

He moved his hands to cover his nipples and lifted the breast tissue to show Niall. He didn't want to look at Niall's face. He knew what he was seeing. Small white scars, some thin and barely noticeable, others thick and raised. "I used to try to cut them off." Cohen dropped his hands and turned away again, leaning over the sink. "It's fine, it's normal. I'm going to get the surgery as soon as I can."

Niall took a few steps forward, then dipped down to pick up Cohen's nightshirt and hand it to him. "How long have you been doing this?"

Cohen took the shirt gratefully and pulled it over his head, then crossed his arms over his chest again. The cut was bleeding through the fabric. He'd have to bandage it properly. "I thought I'd stopped. Guess I'm under a lot of stress."

"I'm so sorry, Cohen." Niall's eyes were wide and open, his sincerity heartbreaking.

"Don't worry about it," said Cohen. "It's fine, okay? It's just something I have to live with." He stooped to pick up the knife from where it had fallen to the floor. He turned the tap on again and rinsed the blood from the tip. "My mam used to hide all the knives at night, because I did it so often. I guess I'll have to start doing that again."

"I'll stop you next time," said Niall. "I'm sorry. I should have stopped you right away."

"You didn't know what I was doing," sighed Cohen, drying off the knife with a dish towel. His heartbeat was still erratic, and he felt sick to his stomach. He pressed a hand to his face to find that the skin was cold and clammy. "I should have a shower," he said. "Um, this is selfish, but do you think you'd mind staying up with me a bit? I just, I don't think I can sleep just yet."

He couldn't find any bandages in the bathroom cupboard, so he settled for holding a cloth over the cut until it stopped bleeding. It was a fairly shallow one; Niall had interrupted him before he'd had a chance to do much damage. Some of the worst incidents had landed him in the hospital. He'd been lucky this time.

He felt angry and ashamed. It had been years since he'd cut. He'd worked through all this in therapy; he was *better*. He didn't want to hate his body. He wanted to embrace it as his own and be patient and let medicine make it into something that felt right. Why was that so hard?

He showered, making sure to wash off all the sweat, and by the end he felt much better, especially when he put his binder back on under a fresh T-shirt. He stared at himself in the mirror for several minutes, drinking in the sight of his flat chest. The relief was almost euphoric. He hoped Niall would be willing to stay up with him. He didn't want to have to take the binder off and go back to sleep. Not for a while.

Niall built the fire up again, and they slipped into bed together. Cohen sat nestled in Niall's arms, staring at the flickering purple flames and the sparks of gold magic that jumped off.

"Niall," he said finally. "Do you think you could use magic to make me...you know, cis?"

"No," said Niall. "I wouldn't dare. I don't know my magic nearly well enough. I could hurt you really badly."

Cohen shifted, his stomach squirming. He had to know. "But I mean, with all the magic out there, there must be someone who could do it."

"There probably is," agreed Niall. "But it'd be a really dangerous procedure, and very expensive as well, and whoever did it would belong to the Guild, so you'd be in their debt. But—" He sighed, and Cohen felt like he waited forever. "—yes, it's possible."

Cohen's heart leapt into his throat. It was possible. He could make his dysphoria go away. He could be normal like everyone else, never have to worry about how he looked to other people, or how wrong his body felt. And he could have sex. But the squirming in his stomach was still there. There was something wrong with that idea; something indescribably horrible about it. "I don't know if I want that though," he said. "I don't know why, but it feels like this is part of who I am."

"You're braver than me," said Niall sadly. "If I could go back in time and make it so I'd never gotten these powers, I would. If I was brave enough, I'd summon that demon right now and ask him to take them away. But you"—he turned to look at Cohen—"you do so much with what you have. You tell your story, and you inspire people."

"But you could do so much too," said Cohen. Niall's face fell, and Cohen almost wished he hadn't said it. Almost.

Niall turned away. "I couldn't. I'm a coward."

"You're not." Cohen shook his head vehemently. "The stakes are huge for you." It was true. Niall could die; he could be captured and tortured. And Cohen? What was stopping him from doing what he wanted? "Niall," he said, "this might be kind of out of the blue, but I kind of want to try having sex again."

Niall looked like he welcomed the distraction. "What, right now?"

Cohen nodded.

"Are...will you be okay? I don't want to make you uncomfortable again."

"Uncomfortable is just going to be part of it," said Cohen. "But I want to do it anyway. This is my body, and I'm stuck with it this way. I don't want to miss out on anything just because it might make me uncomfortable. I have—" He could feel his cheeks colouring slightly. "Well, I brought my strap-on because I was afraid my family might find it in my room while I was away."

Niall laughed at that. He looked at Cohen for a moment, bit his lip. "Yeah," he said finally. "Yeah, I'd love to; just let me get cleaned up."

"Okay." Cohen watched Niall go into the bathroom, excited, and then realised he needed to get ready too. He was buzzing with anticipation, terrified of the dysphoria this was probably going to cause, and determined to ride it out.

He pulled his pyjama pants off and quickly changed into a set of briefs while Niall was in the bathroom. Then he dug through his luggage and pulled out a black plastic bag. Inside was his strap-on and an old bottle of lube. They were the only sex paraphernalia he owned, bought for him by his first girlfriend, who had been several years older than him. He got embarrassed just thinking of what his parents would do if they found out Cohen had this sort of thing.

The strap-on was black, long, and quite realistic looking. Cohen had missed wearing it. He secured the thick polyester straps into place and wrapped his hand around the shaft to position it. He slid his fist up and down the soft silicone a few times, and his imagination did the rest. It wasn't as good as a real one would have been, of course, but it was something.

He was tightening it a little more, making sure the base was pressing up against his real (although notably smaller) cock perfectly, when Niall came back into the room. He was naked, and Cohen could feel the blush rising all the way to the top of his head.

"What do you think?" he asked, laughing through the mortification, and gave the dildo a little push, so that it bounced from side to side. "You can still change your mind." He said it as a joke, but part of him was sceptical that Niall was actually going to go through with this.

Niall just smiled. He walked quickly towards Cohen, the firelight rippling on his skin, and pulled Cohen into a deep kiss. Niall's desperate desire was back, and Cohen happily gave in, opening his mouth to allow their tongues to collide and moaning as Niall's body pressed into his.

Niall's hands were around Cohen's waist already, and Cohen easily slipped his onto Niall's, loving the feel of his hard, angular body. He ran his hands over his hips and thighs, into the soft down of the hair between his legs. He broke away abruptly, breathless, and whispered, "I'm going to touch you now."

Niall's reply was another encouraging kiss, so Cohen slowly drew his hand up Niall's thigh and connected with the soft length there. It was hardening already, and Cohen began to move his hand over it, exploring its shape, the soft head and little folds of skin. It felt easy, somehow, as if he had been used to touching one all along.

"God," he whispered as a surge of lust ran through him, accompanied by a bit of pain at the knowledge that he would never get to do this for himself.

"Are you all right?" asked Niall, breaking their kiss and touching a hand to Cohen's cheek. Cohen had to give him credit for looking concerned even when he was obviously flushed with lust.

"I'm fine," said Cohen, and Niall kissed him again. It was hard to think about anything when Niall was kissing him like that, and Cohen was lost to the feeling of Niall's soft, pliant tongue and hard body, his cock straightening and filling out as Cohen pumped it. Together they stumbled over to the bed, and Cohen, in a moment of confidence, pushed Niall down and straddled him, kissing him and running his hands over him once again.

They kissed for what seemed like an eternity, neither of them interested in rushing things. Niall's hands mostly remained on Cohen's back, sometimes dragging down to touch the backs of his thighs or brush over his ass. Cohen was exploring Niall's body thoroughly, with his hands first, and then his mouth. It was surprisingly similar to being with a girl, and Cohen felt relaxed and confident. He loved flicking his tongue over Niall's nipples, running it between the muscles of his stomach and over his hips.

Eventually, he worked his way between Niall's legs, and Niall automatically lifted his knees and spread his legs. Cohen ran his fingers up Niall's thighs, over his balls, and down to the puckered skin underneath.

"You all right with this?" he confirmed.

Niall nodded. "I trust you."

"Can we do it this way, or should you turn over?"

"This way is fine."

"Okay." Cohen smiled. "Good, I want to look at you."

He moved away for a moment to grab the lube, secretly feeling a little nervous. "You've done this before, right?" he asked Niall, turning back as he rubbed lube between his fingers.

Niall was lying with his head back and didn't respond right away. "Yeah, yeah. Jacky and I..." he trailed off.

Cohen flinched, moving closer again. "I'm sorry. I didn't mean to dredge up bad memories."

Niall sat up a little, shrugging. "You're different from him. I thought what we had was good, but..." He was staring off into the distance now, his eyes lidded. "You know, looking back, I don't think he was that kind to me. I'm sure he loved me, but I don't know if he *cared* about me."

"I care about you," Cohen reassured him. "I only want to do this if you do."

"I do," said Niall, his gaze finally snapping back to the present. "You don't know. I've wanted it for so long, I—" He laughed and ducked his head. "Sorry, never mind."

"No, what?" Cohen pestered him, laughing along with Niall. "What is it?"

"You know I used to watch your videos, sometimes, right?" said Niall. "Like, they'd let me go on the internet sometimes, and then once I escaped, I watched all of them, and I read your books. I... I sort of had a huge crush on you."

"Well, now you've met me, so I'm sure that's killed it dead." Cohen laughed, a little excited by Niall's admonition despite himself.

"Not exactly," said Niall with a grin, and then he leaned forward to kiss Cohen again. "Sort of," he said between kisses. "I'd say...the exact opposite, actually, oh!"

Cohen had passed a wet finger over his opening and, encouraged by Niall's reaction, did it again, firmer this time. Niall leaned back, and Cohen moved forward and began to finger him properly, one hand on Niall's cock, and the other moving in and out in a hooked motion. "This is right, right?" he confirmed. "This is how you do girls."

"Wouldn't know," grunted Niall. "But yeah, that's good. Oh!"

A brilliant excitement was buzzing through Cohen. He'd forgotten how much he loved giving pleasure. He could keep doing this forever, but Niall was looking up at him with eyes dark and desperate.

"Cohen, please," he whispered, and Cohen hurriedly lubed the dildo, sliding his hands over the length. The base bumped against him, sending a shudder of dysphoria through his legs to combat the excitement, but Cohen steadfastly ignored it. He pumped the dildo a few more times, forcing himself to adapt to the feeling, forget what the base was pressing against, focus on what the tip was pressing into.

"Go slow, okay?" Niall asked. "It's been a long time." He was propped up on his elbows, his body a gorgeous taut bow of sinews and muscles, and he tilted his head back as Cohen began to press inwards, revealing the long lines of his throat and the bobbing lump of his Adam's apple. "Oh, god yes..." he moaned as Cohen leaned forward, his hands on Niall's hips for balance.

Cohen pressed his legs together as waves of lust washed through him at the sight of Niall like that. He leaned forward, wanting to be closer to Niall, and the dildo slipped in fully. Niall moaned, and Cohen thought for a moment he was in pain, but then Niall's hands clamped around Cohen's arms, and he pulled Cohen on top of him, wrapping his legs tightly around Cohen's hips.

Their faces were close enough to kiss again, and Cohen took advantage of it. Their tongues tangled together, inside mouths and along lips, and Cohen moved his hips, shoving in and out of Niall. He was out of practice, tiring quickly, but Niall was doing a lot of the work with his legs anyway. Niall's cock was hard against Cohen's stomach; Cohen could feel it through the fabric of his T-shirt. He rubbed against it a little as he fucked, and Niall moaned into his mouth.

"God, I'm going to come, Cohen."

"Mm." Cohen pushed through to his second wind and continued fucking. The slight readjustment had caused the base of the dildo to press into him perfectly, and suddenly he didn't need to make any conscious movements, his body had taken over, desperate for more of that rocking pressure. "Mm! Niall!" he gasped, lifting himself up a little on his arms, and continued moving his hips. His face contorted with pleasure, and the noises escaping his mouth were out of his control. The tip of Niall's cock was still pressing into his stomach, hard and a little wet now. Cohen wanted to reach down and touch it, but he didn't want to risk losing that delicious pressure on his cock.

Niall did it for him, reaching down to pump himself as Cohen climaxed, holding the dildo deep inside Niall for as long as possible. Niall came a second later, spurting hot liquid onto Cohen's shirt and stomach. His body completely spent, Cohen collapsed onto Niall, and they lay gasping together.

Cohen thought maybe he ought to say something, or move, but for a long time, just lying there with Niall was all he wanted. Niall seemed to think the same thing because he didn't say anything either, just lay quietly, stroking Cohen's hair and staring off into the distance again.

Finally Cohen's leg began to cramp a little, and he pulled back, sliding the dildo out of Niall. Niall smiled at him, and Cohen thought he was probably fully aware of how sexy he looked, spent and sticky and open.

They took showers separately, Cohen not sure he was quite ready to be naked with Niall yet. But he put another T-shirt on (his third for the night) without his binder. He'd felt quite dysphoric through the whole process of cleaning off, and throughout the sex as well, really. But it had absolutely been worth it.

Niall dimmed the fire and then set up some sort of spell on the door to wake him if Cohen tried to sleepwalk, and then he came to bed, curling his body around Cohen's and snuggling close. For a while he was so quiet Cohen thought he had fallen asleep. Then he stirred and said, "I'm going to talk to Jacky again after work tomorrow. You're right; I can't just stand by and do nothing."

Cohen felt his blood run cold. "No," he said instinctively. "I don't want you to. What if he tries to hurt you?"

"Then I'll try to hurt him back," said Niall simply. "I can take care of myself."

Cohen sniffed and snuggled closer to Niall. He didn't like this one bit. He really had gotten himself involved in something bad. He was falling for a man who was in danger of dying. Was this what it was like to be married to a soldier? He didn't like it. He wanted Niall safe. He wanted to spend the last of his savings to cart him off to somewhere, and leave all this behind. But he'd been the one who had told Niall that he couldn't just run away.

"You're brave," he told Niall, and Niall scoffed quietly.

"I'm really not. I'm a coward. Complacent."

"You're kind."

"I suppose that's true. Too kind."

"Maybe a little." Cohen laughed.

Niall turned to face Cohen and pressed their lips together in a soft kiss, devoid of any of the desperation of earlier. This one lingered, sweet, as if he didn't want the moment to end. Finally it did, and Niall took Cohen's face in his hands. "I don't know what's going to happen to me," he said. "But I want you to know that I think you're brilliant. And I hope—" He broke off, but Cohen thought he knew what he'd been going to say.

"I hope so too," he said. "I'm glad I met you."

They fell asleep at last, with Niall's arms locked around Cohen. Cohen's dreams were a confused mixture of excitement and desperation and fear, held at bay only by the warmth of Niall next to him and the memory of his hot, fervent kisses.

Chapter Eight

Cohen woke earlier than Niall, and he slipped out of bed quietly, careful not to wake him. The spells that Niall had set up seemed to be able to tell whether or not he was sleepwalking, because they let him leave the room without incident. He made a stop at his luggage to grab the little black case and headed to the bathroom with it. He was supposed to do his shot tonight, but he couldn't wait any longer.

He pulled the syringe out and began the process, drawing the thick clear liquid into the barrel, and then switching the needle for a long, thinner one. He remembered the first few times he'd done this, he'd been shaky and unsure. Now it was second nature. Pulling off his pyjama trousers, he sat on the toilet lid in his briefs and wiped the spot on his thigh with steriliser.

Drawing in a deep breath, he positioned the long needle directly over his leg, and with a long exhale, stabbed downwards. The needle entered effortlessly, and Cohen forced himself to stay relaxed. There was a sting, and the inevitable reaction of confusion and upset from his body. The light above him was a little too bright, and his heart was beating fast. Taking another long breath, he gripped the barrel and slowly pushed the plunger down. He wanted to do it quickly, to get it over with, but he forced his hand to move slowly and surely. When the needle was empty at last, he pulled it out of his leg with a swift motion, and set it on the counter next to him.

Done. He was good for two weeks. The relief washed through him. He knew it wouldn't be taking effect yet, but he already felt better. He cleaned up, wiping everything down with more steriliser and disposing of the needles in the special bin he'd brought, before pulling his trousers back on and then heading back into the bedroom.

Niall was awake when he returned, sitting up and watching curiously as Cohen returned the case to its place amongst his clothes. "Are you going to have to do that for the rest of your life?" he asked.

"Probably." Cohen sighed, slipping into the bed with Niall. It had been cold in the bathroom, but Niall had kept the bed nice and warm. "Which is a pain because I want to travel and live in different countries. I don't like being limited to where I can easily access my meds."

Niall leaned over him and kissed him lightly. Cohen took a deep, shaky breath and kissed him back. Niall's warmth was slowly pushing the shivers and cold away. "Where do you want to go?" asked Niall.

"I'm not sure yet," Cohen admitted. "I know I want somewhere I can be independent. My parents don't know it, but this trip was sort of a test run, to see how I could handle living on my own, to figure out exactly what I wanted."

"What have you figured out, then?"

"Hmm." Cohen snuggled in closer to Niall, thinking. "Well, I know I don't want a small town. I think I'm a city lad at heart. I wanted to go somewhere no one knew who I was, but I think you get more anonymity in a big city. And I..." He paused. He'd wanted to be alone. He'd felt put upon, with his family, like he never had any privacy or space. But he was with someone now, and he didn't feel that way at all. "I thought I wanted to be alone, but maybe I was just waiting for the right person."

"Cohen..." Niall sounded apprehensive.

"Seriously, Niall, think about it." Cohen let his imagination run wild. "I could buy a place somewhere far away; there must be places that the Guild doesn't have much influence. And then once I'm settled in, you could come live with me. No one would know you were there, and you wouldn't have to work or come up with a fake ID or anything."

Niall's face was blank. Cohen looked up at him, waiting for him to respond. "Niall?"

"I don't want to think about it," said Niall. "I'm sorry, Cohen, but I don't want to hope for that sort of thing. If the Guild catch me again, and they take me back there..." He shuddered, and Cohen felt it pass through him as well. "I don't want to have that hope taken away from me. It would kill me."

"We could go right now," said Cohen. "We could leave tonight."

"We can't," said Niall. "And you know that. I have to stop Jacky."

Cohen sighed and settled back into Niall, his fantasy dissipating like mist in sunlight. "Well, it was a nice thought."

"I'll go talk to Jacky tonight," said Niall. "After work. I don't know if I can change his mind, or even get through to him at all, but I have to try. I can't stop trying."

"I'll go with you," said Cohen.

"No!" Niall shook his head violently. "You can't. It's too dangerous. And, anyway, Cohen, listen." He put a hand to Cohen's face and kissed him again. "If," he whispered, "if that plan of yours is going to work out, it's imperative that the Guild not find out that I'm involved with you. Otherwise they'll use you to get to me. Do you understand?"

"I do," said Cohen. He did understand. But he also knew that there were more important things at stake than their future together. That was why they couldn't leave right now, not until Jacky was stopped. And why, if it came down to it, he would have to sacrifice everything to stop him. "But I couldn't live with myself if something bad happened, and I did nothing to stop it."

"You don't need to do anything," said Niall. "Just keep yourself safe."

★

Cohen pushed the small white button firmly and listened as the doorbell echoed throughout the house within. A few seconds later, there was a thumping from indoors and the door flew open.

A teenage girl stood there, her eyes alight. She stared at Cohen for a few moments, then lunged forward and embraced him with a squeal. "Oh my god, it's you!" she squeaked. "I'm your biggest fan!"

"Um." Cohen was torn between the desire to disentangle himself from her long skinny arms and not wanting to offend her. "I guess you're probably Myrna's daughter?"

The girl jumped back and straightened her bobbed black hair nervously. "Yeah!" she squeaked again, breathless. "I'm Kelsie. Sorry." She wrung her long fingers together, and then Myrna's voice boomed from inside the house.

"What are you doing, Kelsie? Invite him in." She appeared at the doorway behind her daughter a few seconds later, looking disgruntled and holding a newspaper. "Glad you could make it," she said with a small smile. "Sorry about my daughter."

"It's okay," said Cohen, trying to smile at Kelsie, who was still wringing her hands and staring at him in awe. "It's nice to meet a fan."

At that, Kelsie's forced reservation dissolved once again, and she pounced on him for another hug.

"Kelsie," said Myrna in a warning tone, and Kelsie backed away.

"I'm sorry, I'm sorry!" Her hands fluttered to her mouth. "It's just I never met another trans person before!"

"You probably have and just didn't know it," said Cohen, a smile creeping onto his face as he realised what she was saying.

"Yeah, but you're the first person I knew about," she said, her face now taking on a slight pink tone. "You're so amazing!"

"I'm not that amazing in real life," Cohen warned her. "I'm just normal."

"Well now, you're slightly amazing," laughed Myrna. "All right, Kelsie, back off and let your sister say hello."

Cohen hadn't even noticed there was another person in the room, a little plump girl with the same frizzy red hair and stern face as Myrna. "Hello," she said solemnly, holding out a hand for Cohen to shake.

Cohen shook it, unable to keep from smiling. "Hello, I'm Cohen. What's your name?"

"I'm Noleen," she intoned. "It's nice to meet you. Kelsie made me watch all your videos."

"Shut up, Pinky!" said Kelsie, looking quite mortified, considering the shameless abandon she had displayed a moment ago.

"Well you did!" said Noleen, sticking her chin out.

"Girls," said Myrna firmly, "go and check on dinner, please."

The girls skittered off to the kitchen, and Myrna gave Cohen a long-suffering look. "I'm sorry about Kelsie," she said, beckoning Cohen into the sitting room. "You see I couldn't *not* invite you to dinner; there'd be a mutiny."

"I understand," said Cohen. When Myrna still looked apologetic, he continued. "It's really okay. I've met other young people like her; I guess I sort of accepted the mentor role when I came out publicly."

"You didn't really have a choice though, did you?" she asked as they sat down.

"Well, I suppose I could have gone into hiding," joked Cohen and then a little more solemnly said, "I suppose I *have.*"

"I'm sorry to drag you out of it," said Myrna apologetically. "But I promise you'll get nothing but support in this house."

"I do need it here," sighed Cohen, thinking of how the people in town had treated him. He'd been afraid to go into town today, preferring to lock himself up at home and attempt to distract himself. Niall had left for work shortly after their conversation, and Cohen had spent the day writing. He'd given up on writing the next book in his series, instead letting his thoughts flow out. Nothing amazing had come of it, but it felt good to be doing it again. And it was the only thing that had kept the anxiety he felt over Niall at bay. Niall must be done working by now. He was probably talking to Jacky. What if he was in danger?

Cohen felt cold dread shoot through him at the thought, despite the warm comfort of Myrna's sitting room. "Sorry," he said, realising he'd trailed off.

Myrna was looking at him strangely. "Has something happened?" she asked. "I mean, besides what you told me?"

"Nothing," said Cohen. "I mean, I saw Niall again last night, but nothing bad happened." *But something horrible might be happening right now.*

"Hmm." Myrna looked a little less than impressed. "I'm not sure I trust that man."

"Oh, I trust him," said Cohen. "I just..." He thought about what Niall had said, that it was better if no one knew about the fact that they were together. He should change the subject. "I was wondering something."

"What's that?"

"It's just a hypothetical question," said Cohen nervously. "Like, for my writing."

"All right," said Myrna, "go on."

"Well it's about morality, really. I mean, I know most people would sacrifice themselves to save other people, right? Especially if it were to save, like, a *lot* of other people."

"Well, yes," said Myrna. "It would be difficult to live with yourself otherwise, wouldn't it? Most people don't even feel they have a choice."

"Right," said Cohen. "That's easy. But what about when saving the lives of a bunch of people depends on you...killing someone else. I'm asking, basically, if you could live with killing one person in order to save the lives of many others. Would it be right?"

Myrna raised her eyebrows. "Your next book is going to be a bit different from your other ones then, I suppose?"

"Maybe a little." Cohen laughed nervously. "I am an adult now."

"Of course," said Myrna. "Well, the answer to that's not simple. It depends on the person. Of course I would do it. But"—she shrugged—"I'm a police officer. It's part of our—or at least my—creed. We give up the luxury of a clear conscience, give up our own moral purity, as it were, for the well-being of other people. It's a sacrifice I chose to make when I joined the police force."

"I guess not everyone's cut out for that," said Cohen, thinking of Niall's reluctance. His softness, the way he was so kind and gentle even after what had happened to him.

"Certainly not," Myrna agreed. "And it's best that way. It...breaks a lot of people, you see. That's why so many officers are corrupt. Having to do bad things for the sake of the greater good, it can—" She paused. "It can make you forget what the greater good is, turn good men into shadows of themselves. So many of the officers in the city were like that. It's one of the reasons I moved out here."

"When did you move?"

"After my husband died," said Myrna. She said it very matter-of-factly, but Cohen thought it was too much so. The lack of emotion in her voice gave it away. "He was a Garda too," she continued. "We worked together, and at one point we got in over our heads, involved in a drug conspiracy. He was killed, and I—" She sighed, and her eyes were distant. "—I thought it might be better to bring the girls out here. Simpler. But I don't know now if I was just being selfish. I think Kelsie might need the city. Of course, I can drive her into the doctor there, but she's rather alone here. There's no one else like her."

"Well." Cohen swallowed. "I understand that, but I also understand wanting to get them out of that kind of environment."

"It *was* mostly for my sake, though," said Myrna, glancing at the door to the kitchen. "I thought it would be peaceful here, that I could heal, and that would be better for them. But of course it's turned out to be just as difficult here, what with the murders."

Cohen thought of Niall again, and the lump in his throat was back.

"And now Kelsie's gone and gotten herself a boyfriend here," said Myrna with a small laugh, turning away from the kitchen to look at Cohen again. "So she'd kill me if I tried to move her now."

★

They had a nice dinner of potatoes and roast beef. It was a loud, chatty affair that reminded Cohen of being back home with his family. Kelsie talked about her boyfriend, and Noleen interjected occasionally to correct her on insignificant details. Noleen also told Cohen, a little shyly when pressed, that she wanted to be a writer when she grew up, and that she liked his books.

Looking past Kelsie's chattiness and enthusiasm, Cohen was reminded of himself at her age, minus his scene hair and interest in girls. And of course, Kelsie mentioned that she was out at school and had seen a doctor and been put on hormone blockers.

"It's all because of you," she told Cohen sincerely. "You inspired me to come out with your video about it last year. I always loved you and your books, and when I saw that video I was so happy. I showed it to my mam and she said, 'Well, if that's how you feel, we'll see someone about it.'"

"I'm not sure I was that accepting at first." Myrna laughed through a bite of potatoes.

"You just explained it so well," said Kelsie to Cohen. "I don't understand how anybody could be mad at you about it after that."

"Well, they were," said Cohen. "But maybe they didn't watch the video. The newspapers were all on it, you know, and they said all sorts of terrible things." He sighed, feeling depressed at the memory.

"Frankly, I don't see why they care so much," said Myrna with a slight scowl. "Didn't think authors were so much in the public eye."

"It's just me," sighed Cohen. "Everyone in Ireland loved me for getting my books on the international market, especially because I was so young. My dad used to tell me I was Ireland's favourite daughter." Kelsie frowned, and Cohen mimicked the expression. "They felt like they owned me, I suppose. Put a black mark on their image."

"What's a black mark?" asked Noleen.

"Something bad," said Myrna. "Well, Cohen, I hope you don't let that get you down. You always seem very positive in your videos."

"I am positive." Cohen smiled again so Kelsie would as well. "I try to be, you know; what else can I do?"

"Well," said Kelsie, looking nervous. "You know you don't have to be all the time. I saw your last video; I think it's good that you're taking some time for yourself. You shouldn't have to pretend to be happy all the time just to make other people happy."

"Well, no," said Cohen. He tilted his head and smiled at Kelsie. "But that's what makes *me* happy."

The rest of the evening was enjoyable and relaxing, but Cohen couldn't shake his nerves about Niall. He tried his best to be good company and engage in conversation though, and if Myrna noticed anything, she didn't say. But by the time the cuckoo clock above the fireplace announced it was nine o'clock, Noleen was ready for bed, and Cohen was anxious to leave.

He pulled over just before he left town, while there were still a few bars of service on his phone, and called Niall's home line, but there was no answer. He called his mobile next, but that one went straight to voicemail, which meant that Niall's phone was either turned off or he was out of service.

Drumming his fingers nervously on the steering wheel, Cohen pulled back onto the road and began the drive home. The sun had just set, and there was a dusty blue tinge to the horizon, although above, the stars glittered brightly, only obscured occasionally by wisps of clouds. The old car didn't like the ups and downs of the hilly countryside, and he had to fight to keep a steady pace, but rather than distract him, it only made his nerves more frayed. He'd begun to chew at his thumbnail again, wondering if he should bother going home or just keep driving around until he found Niall, when a flash lit the horizon, so quick he almost missed it.

Cohen gripped the steering wheel once again and leaned over to peer out at the skyline. Lightning? But the sky was calm. Perhaps he was imagining things. Just when he was beginning to convince himself he hadn't seen anything, there was another flash, this one longer, lighting up the entire sky, and he thought he saw a swirl of bright white fire in it.

He could feel the hairs on the back of his neck tickling in a way he was beginning to recognise. *Magic*. He took a turn-off to a smaller road that ducked behind a hill in the direction of the lights. Nerves buzzing, Cohen followed it a ways, then pulled over to the side of the road and stepped out of the car, peering over at the nearest hill to the east. Was there anything over there? Myrna had said there were stone circles to the north, near his house, like Stonehenge. And Niall had said something about Druids.

He locked the car door hurriedly and shoved his lanyard into his pocket, pulling his coat around himself and stepping off the road into the ankle-high grass. It was wet with evening dew, and his shoes were soon soaked, but he didn't care. He knew he should leave well enough alone, and this was dangerous, but if something bad was happening, he couldn't just drive on and ignore it. He walked a bit quicker, coming to a fence at the base of the hill, and managed to climb over it, landing heavily in a pile of mud.

"Uck," he muttered, wiping his shoes off on the grass. There was another flash of light, and this time a muffled boom as well, and then another flash; he felt a tingling wind brush by his face, like an aftershock. He started up the hill, breathing heavily by the time he came to the top. There was another dip and a smaller hill up ahead. He could see the lights clearly now, flashes and booms, and the occasional blinding flare that jumped up to the sky in a burst of searing white flame. Cohen took a deep breath. His heart was racing, and he could feel his sporadic pulse at the base of his throat.

Boom. Muted, as if very far away, despite the closeness of the lights. He rushed forward and almost tripped over a pile of sticks and rocks. He turned to examine them, a row of carefully placed materials, and he recognised them instantly as similar to the wards Niall had placed all over his house. His hand crept to the talisman hanging from the string around his neck, and another shivering prickle ran up his spine.

Boom. This one was much louder, with enough force to nearly knock Cohen off his feet. The searing light that shot up into the sky was right over the hill, and he could feel the heat and buzz, like electricity, radiating from it. Hurriedly, he rushed back over the line of wards, and the lights were dimmed again, the sound strangely muted.

A ward. It was a ward to keep magic from getting out. The line of talismans must run in a circle all the way around, so any magic done inside the line couldn't be tracked. That made sense, right? Cohen gulped and jumped over the line again, rushing up the hill. This was so, so stupid. He was going to be killed, and it was going to be entirely his own fault. He should go back to his car and drive to the Coughton and stay there, where it was safe, until morning. But he *couldn't*.

He continued up the hill, nearly out of breath before he reached the crest and stared at the scene ahead. There were standing stones, tall and black against the blue of the sky, but illuminated in blasts by white light. Two figures stood amongst them, darting towards each other and away again, searing, sparkling white flames bursting towards each other. Mostly they dodged out of the way, but sometimes the flames would collide, and that would cause the deafening boom and the explosion of white fire towards the sky.

"Jacky!" a voice yelled, and with a lurch of his gut, Cohen recognised it as Niall's. "Jacky, stop it!"

The other man was laughing, as if it were all great fun, even when the searing light he shot at Niall barely missed him and scorched the grass where Niall had been a moment before. Cohen could see the embers of the grass that remained, glowing and sizzling in the darkness. "You think I'm just going to let you ruin everything?" he called as Niall ducked behind one of the stones. "You think it'll all stop just because you tell me you love me? You don't love me anymore. I saw!"

Another blast, and this one connected with the upright stone. It crumbled and began to fall.

"Niall!" Cohen screamed before he could stop himself, and suddenly Niall was in front of him, his eyes wide.

"Cohen, what are you doing here?"

"I'm sorry, I saw flashes of light, so I—"

"You need to go," said Niall, and he all but shoved at Cohen. "Go, run, now!"

"Too late," said a voice. "Why don't you introduce me, Niall?" Jacky was suddenly next to them and advancing on Cohen. Cohen couldn't see his face very well in the dark, only the long, matted hair and glinting eyes. "Is this your lover?"

Niall stepped forward to come between Cohen and Jacky. "He's not," he said firmly.

"I'm not?" asked Cohen, fear making him stupid.

"Cohen," said Niall, still facing Jacky. "Shut up. Leave, right now."

Jacky peered around Niall to grin at Cohen. "You are, aren't you?" He tilted his head to indicate Niall. "His mind is full of you. Cohen, isn't it? You will be so very useful to me." He took a step forward, and Niall moved between them again.

"Cohen," said Niall again. "When I say so, run."

"That's not happening—" began Jacky, but he was interrupted as Niall shot a swatch of crackling magic at him.

"Run!" Niall shouted as Jacky threw up his hands and retaliated. The light was so bright and the noise so loud that, for a moment, Cohen couldn't see or hear anything but the terrible boom and blinding light. Sparks of magic burst behind his eyes, and he could hardly tell up from down, but he could hear Niall yelling, so he turned and ran.

He tripped; the hill was steeper than he had thought it was, and he landed heavily on his shoulder. Disoriented, he began to roll. The grass was wet under his palms as he grasped at it, and he was hitting his shoulder over and over again as he fell, sending shots of pain through him until he thought he might be sick.

He stopped rolling finally, the wind taken out of him, but he could see flashes of light and could hear Niall still yelling at him. "Run, get out of the circle!" Cohen forced himself to get up, trying desperately to regain his balance, to figure out which way was which. He nearly fell and assumed that was downwards, so he began to run again, his trainers slipping and squeaking on the wet grass.

He tripped again, over the line of sticks and rocks, and then Niall was there, holding on to him to keep him from falling again. *Safe.* They were safe, right? He had just begun to get his wind back when there was another flash and Niall was shoving him again, just in time to get out of the way of a searing burst of magic.

"He can't use magic outside of the circle," gasped Niall. "Come on, Cohen, run." He shoved at Cohen again, and Cohen ran, unsure of where he was getting the air since his lungs seemed to have stopped working. His throat was burning, his heart about to pound out of his chest. The wind whipped by his face, and he could hear footsteps behind him. Suddenly Niall's presence was gone from beside him, and he turned to see Niall standing between him and Jacky once again.

"You can't do anything now, Jacky," he was saying. "We're outside the circle; they'll track it."

Jacky was out of breath, too, and laughing through gasps. He lifted a hand, and the last thing Cohen saw was a flash of light, burning as Niall screamed.

Cohen felt his body thump to the ground, his head whacking against the dirt. His temple began to throb angrily, and he groaned. "Cohen!" Niall screamed, rushing to bend over him. He touched a hand to Cohen's chest and drew it back as if burnt. Cohen looked down just in time to see an orange glow dying down into a black scorch mark in the middle of his chest. He lifted a hand to his neck, where there was a strange burning, but felt only a crumbling warm dust. When he brought his fingers away, they were coated in black ash.

"The talisman," he whispered. Niall gave him a look of relief and then stood to face Jacky again.

"You idiot!" he yelled. "You did that outside your bloody circle; they'll know where we are now!"

Jacky grinned. Cohen could see his teeth, white in the darkness. "What's wrong with that?" he laughed. "You saw my mind, Niall, so you know what I need: father, child, sage, *lover*—" He glanced at Cohen. "—*witch*. Ha!" He threw a hand in the air, and a blinding white light erupted from it, crackling and swooping like a great bonfire. It shot into the air, reaching a dizzying height, and Cohen felt the hairs all over his body standing up and tingling. Jacky took another step towards Niall. "I'm almost finished," he said. "So get out of my way."

Niall growled and turned towards Cohen, who was just beginning to stand. He threw his arms around Cohen and grasped his head, pulling it to his chest. "Hold still, darling," he whispered to Cohen. "I've never done this before."

A bright white light exploded around them, and for a moment, Cohen felt like all the air had been sucked out of his lungs and he was suffocating. There was nothing beneath his feet, nothing in front of his eyes, only Niall's arms around him. Then they landed heavily, and Niall's arms loosened. Cohen nearly fell sideways, and Niall caught him.

"What the hell did you come after me for?" he growled at Cohen, releasing him roughly once Cohen had caught his balance. Cohen pressed his hands to his eyes to try to stop the white lights flashing behind them. His head was pounding. "Come on, this way."

Cohen blinked, clearing the spots from behind his eyes, to see that they were back on the road. His car was nowhere in sight, but Niall's truck was close by. Niall was gesturing to him. "Come on, Cohen, get in. They'll have tracked that; we have to get away from this location."

"How far away?" asked Cohen, stumbling towards the truck.

"We'll go to your house for now," said Niall. "They won't know to look there. Not right away, anyway."

"Okay." Cohen almost failed to pull himself up into the cab of the truck. His limbs were shaking, his hands unable to grasp anything properly. He thumped down onto the seat and felt sick again. His head was throbbing from when he'd hit the ground, and he was beginning to feel a scorching pain on his neck and chest from where the necklace had been incinerated.

He took several deep breaths, mentally surveying his body for injuries. Nothing was unbearably painful, so he didn't think there was any lasting damage, but he felt like shit. His whole body began to ache as he settled into the seat, but it was all secondary to the intense throbbing in his head.

"I think I may have a concussion," he whined. "I hit my head when I fell."

"You're lucky that's all," said Niall softly.

Cohen cracked an eye open and peered at Niall, who was driving with his eyes forward and his jaw tight. Cohen closed his eyes again and leaned his head back, trying to think.

"He tried to kill me!" he burst out, and immediately flinched from the noise of his own voice.

"Hmm," said Niall, staring forward.

"He—why?"

"Because you shouldn't have been there." Niall shot a withering glare at Cohen. "I *told* you to stay out of it."

Cohen sighed sharply and leaned forward. He felt like his body was creaking. "All right, fine; you're mad at me. I was stupid, but you can't expect me to just sit by and let you get hurt. You need to tell me what's going on. Did he really see into your mind?"

"Yeah," said Niall. He leaned forward as he turned a corner, and then sat back again, his arm held straight and gripping the steering wheel. "I saw his too though; that was kind of the point. He just got past my defences. But at least I know what he's doing now."

He was silent again, staring at the road.

"Well?" prompted Cohen. "Go on."

Niall made an exasperated noise and glared at Cohen again. "Cohen, I told you I didn't want you involved in this!"

"Then you shouldn't have picked me up at the train station!"

"I know that!" Niall shouted and Cohen slumped back, cowed by his outburst. "And believe me, I'm sorry I did."

"Well," said Cohen, trying and failing not to take Niall's claim personally. "That's stupid. You'd be in jail if you hadn't, and you wouldn't have been able to stop him anyway."

"That's what he wants." Niall sighed. "He wanted to set me up for the murders, so I'd get put in jail and be out of the way. The police have a record that I was involved with you, so if you're dead, I'm obviously going to be the prime suspect. Again." He gritted his teeth.

"So that's why he tried to kill me," confirmed Cohen.

"No." Niall shook his head. "I mean, yes, but there's more. I saw in his head; the Druids set up a ritual for the release of the Titan. The need has to be great enough that you're willing to sacrifice people for it. I already knew that, but it looks like there are specific people that have to be sacrificed."

"That's what he was going on about: *father, child—*"

"*Sage, lover, witch*," finished Niall. "He killed a father, a child, and then your lawyer. Took their hearts and sacrificed them. I saw the altar."

Cohen shuddered. "So it's just lover and witch."

"And now he's got specific ones in mind for them," said Niall. "He wants Kathleen for the witch. I saw it in his head; he's hell-bent on using her, getting his revenge that way. He's—" He gritted his teeth. "He's getting emotional, getting stuck on ideas. He does that. He needs it to be Kathleen; that's why he did magic outside of the circle, so she'd know where we are and come."

"But he doesn't have the lover yet."

"He's running out of time; he has to do them by the full moon. He *thought* he had the lover. He was going to use you."

"But—" Cohen jerked forward, earning another throb of pain from his head. "He doesn't need to use me! He could get any lover; all he has to do is sacrifice them before Kathleen gets here. Niall, you have to stop him."

Niall swallowed. "I told you; he gets bent on ideas. I think he's probably stuck on the lover being you."

"You *think*?" said Cohen. "Did you see that in his head, or are you just guessing?"

"I'm just guessing, but I know him."

"Niall, that's not good enough. He could be out there killing someone right now! You need to go stop him!"

"What, and just leave you here?" Niall gestured, and Cohen realised that Niall had pulled up in front of the Coughton. "What if he's coming after you? I have to protect you!"

"You have to protect me because you're absolutely sure it's me he's after?" asked Cohen. "Or because you think he *might* be after me, and you'd rather protect me than save everyone else?"

"Cohen—"

"You need to answer me, Niall."

"We need to get inside." Niall opened his door and jumped out, slamming it behind him. Cohen fumbled with his seat belt and jumped out after him.

"Niall!" Cohen ran after Niall, grabbing his arm and tugging him back to look at him. "Answer me."

"I don't know, all right?" said Niall through gritted teeth. "I don't know anything except I don't want to lose you."

I don't want to lose me either!" said Cohen. He could feel his eyes wide with fear, and his body was shaking. "I am terrified right now, but there are more important things than me."

"I know." Niall shut his eyes for a long moment. Then he opened them again and pulled Cohen into a kiss. Cohen felt himself melt into him, and he wanted to get away, just leave with Niall, go somewhere they would be safe, forget everything else. "I just can't do this."

"You have to," said Cohen. They couldn't run away. Not from this.

"What if I leave you here and he comes after you?"

"He doesn't know where I am, does he? He doesn't know where I live."

"He can find out, Cohen. You're not safe alone."

"Well then." Cohen's heart sank into his gut. His head was throbbing again, and all he wanted to do was sleep. "I have to stay with you. It's the only way to keep me safe."

Niall nodded. "All right. But I'm getting you another talisman. Then we'll try and see if we can find him. But I can't promise we will."

"We have to try," said Cohen.

"I know."

Chapter Nine

"Where are you going?" Warren looked up at Kathleen as she stood suddenly, shoving the chair back with a screech. "Are you all right?"

"Fine." She waved a hand at him distractedly. "Fine, fine, I just need some air."

"Well." He glanced from Kathleen back to Mina. She lay in the hospital bed, asleep for now, though the tubes feeding into her nose and mouth made her sleep restless. "Don't be long."

"I know. I won't be." *Breathe.* She had to breathe. She left the room quickly, her heels clacking on the linoleum floor, and stepped out into the hallway, taking deep breaths of sour-tasting air. She leaned up against the wall and turned her head to the side, her eyes locking onto the red-painted fire alarm next to her face without really seeing it at all.

For a moment her mind went blank, and all she could do was stare and breathe. Then she snapped back to reality and turned, before striding back into the hospital room.

"Everything all right?" asked Warren as she reached for her purse and pulled out her mobile.

"Yes, fine," she said again, pulling up the contact number and dialling. "I've got to go though. I... I remembered something about work."

"You remembered something about work?" Warren stood up to look at her, his tone disgusted and his face full of betrayal. "Kathleen, what could possibly be more important than this?"

"It's just something I remembered. I have to try—"

He strode up to her and took her face in his hands. She had finished dialling, and she could hear ringing on the other side. "Kathleen, please don't. They let you go, remember? They won't help us anymore."

"I—" Her face twisted, and she fought back tears. "I have to go."

"Don't," he whispered. "It's over. There's nothing we can do for her now except be here."

Her phone clicked and a tinny voice answered, "Hello?"

"Yes." Kathleen lifted the phone to her face and tore herself away from Warren. He lifted his arms as she left and held them in the air in a gesture of helplessness.

"Kathleen!" he shouted as she swept out of the room, and she heard him make a wordless cry of outrage and desperation. She wished he wouldn't. He would wake Mina.

"H-hello," she said, attempting to mask the shakiness of her voice with professionalism. "It's Kathleen Singh. I'm picking up something on my instruments."

"Yes," sighed the man on the other end. "We've picked it up as well. I'm sending a team out."

"No!" She shoved her way into the stairwell, all but running down the stairs. "It's my responsibility. I'll take care of it."

"Singh, you no longer work for us actively. Do you recall?"

"So bring me back in." There was silence on the other end. She finished descending and slammed the door open, stepping outside. "Craske!"

Craske sighed. "Fine, Singh, you have two days to locate the fugitives and bring them in. I'm only allowing this because you were my best operative, and I trust your methods. If they disappear again, there will be hell to pay, and I mean that."

"I understand, sir."

There was a call waiting. She hung up on Craske and checked the call display. It was Warren. She pulled her keys out of her pocket and unlocked her car, then slid into the driver's seat and stared at the picture on the screen. Warren was pretending to smile in it. He was good at it, but she always knew. She hung up and started the car.

★

They drove for hours, up and down every street in Witton, until Cohen could have sworn he'd memorised them all. Eventually, he began to nod off, his head slumping against the seat belt, his hand clutching Niall's for reassurance. He knew he should keep his eyes open, stare into the darkness ahead and around, but it was so very difficult. He didn't know how long he'd been asleep when Niall suddenly slammed on the brakes. Cohen jerked forward, the seat belt locking and thumping him backwards. His head throbbed. "Ow," he whispered, touching a hand to the back of his head where a lump was forming. "What is it?"

"Shh," said Niall. "I think I saw something." He pointed ahead. A walkway led into a wooded park next to an old, dark house. "I think..." He pursed his lips, peering into the darkness. "I'm going to check it out," he said finally. "Stay here."

"Are you kidding? I'm coming with you in case someone tries to kill me."

Niall sighed. "Fine." He opened the door and jumped out. "Quiet," he said, shutting the door gently, and Cohen copied him.

Niall reached to grab Cohen's hand as they walked, through trees and down a dark path. It was dark enough that Cohen could barely see Niall's face, and the shadows were inky black. They might have been full of demons and Cohen would never know.

The wind picked up again and Cohen heard a snap. "What was that?" he squeaked, swinging his head around.

"Cohen!" shouted Niall, and suddenly Cohen felt leaves and branches tangling around his arms and legs. Something hard and alive wound around him, lifting him off the ground, and a heavy branch slipped around his middle, painfully tight. He screamed Niall's name, but more branches crept across his face, and the bitter taste of leaves filled his mouth. He yelled, the sound muffled, and tears came to his eyes. He tried not to struggle, not to panic. God, he was going to die; he was going to suffocate!

Niall screamed Cohen's name again and lunged at the branches, trying to pull them off with his bare hands, and then with burning magic, his hands flaming but failing to burn anything but Cohen. The tree gripped him tighter, and Cohen gave a muffled scream of pain.

"You'll only make it worse that way," said a voice, and Niall whipped around, magical fire pulsing from his hands. Cohen saw his eyes go wide and strained to see the figure who had spoken. It was a woman.

"Kathleen," said Niall, and he faltered and took a step back. "Let him go!"

Mercifully, the branches around Cohen began to loosen, and the leaves receded from his mouth. Cohen coughed, desperately drawing in ragged breaths. There was a pain in his chest and his mouth felt dry. He turned his head to see Kathleen, and in the light glowing from Niall's hands, he saw a small and delicate woman, her white-blonde hair pulled back from her face, and her expression hard. She was dressed more like a businesswoman than a witch.

She tilted her head at Niall's glowing hands. "Put that away."

"Why?" hissed Niall. "No point in hiding it now; you know where I am."

"Well, yes," said Kathleen. "But if you try to fight me, I will kill him." She nodded in Cohen's direction, and Cohen felt the branches tighten around his middle again. He tried not to struggle, not to panic.

Niall was breathing heavily through his nose. "Fine," he said. "Let him go, and I won't fight you. But"—he took a step forward—"you need to listen to me. Jacky is going to do something terrible, and we have to stop him."

Kathleen's eyes narrowed. "What?"

"I saw into his mind," said Niall. "He wants to destroy the Guild. He's summoning something to do it."

"And why should I believe you?"

"I'm telling the truth," said Niall. He let his hands drop to his sides, and the glow disappeared, leaving them all in darkness. "You can look in my mind, if you want."

"Maybe I will," said Kathleen. "I've trained myself, you know. You won't take my mind again."

"I don't want to," said Niall. "I'm telling the truth, I swear."

"He is," said Cohen. His voice sounded weak and thin in the darkness. Kathleen turned her head to look at him for a moment.

"Fine," she said finally. She uncrossed her arms and took a step towards Niall, lifting her hands to touch either side of his face. For a moment there was silence, and then she stepped back with a *tsk*.

"That boy's mind is a mad house."

"He's troubled," said Niall, and Kathleen laughed.

"Oh, don't make excuses for him, Niall; we haven't time for that."

"We?" said Niall warily.

"Yes," said Kathleen. "I'm going to need your help to stop him, I think. I'm doing this for my daughter, you know. It's your fault she's dying now. But, if I bring you and Jacky to them, the Guild might take pity on her." She snapped her fingers, and the branches around Cohen began to recede. Niall rushed to Cohen and helped pull the last of them off.

"So you'll help us because if the Guild is destroyed, they won't be able to help your daughter," said Niall. He finished releasing Cohen, who slumped into his arms. Niall felt warm, although his body was stiff, and Cohen clung to him, choking back tears.

"It's in my best interests," said Kathleen, seeming entirely unconcerned with Cohen. "But after this, I am turning you both in, and that's that."

"Well, I'm sorry," said Niall, "but I'm going to run again."

"Yes, I know you are. And I'm going to stop you this time. I swear it."

Cohen coughed. His throat and chest felt raw. He wanted to be home, in his bed, not out in the darkness with killer trees and psycho murderers. Niall finished brushing leaves from Cohen's hair and touched his cheek. "I'm sorry, Cohen; you have to be strong."

"I know, I know," whispered Cohen. "I'm okay."

"Hurry up; we don't have forever." Kathleen was already heading back to the street, and they hurriedly followed her.

"Kathleen," Niall said. "Jacky wants to kill you. He summoned you here because he wants to use you as the last sacrifice."

Kathleen stopped walking and turned to look at them again. "I'm aware."

"I'll try to stop him, is all," said Niall.

"Oh," said Kathleen, and Cohen could see a small smile on her face despite the darkness. "You think that'll make up for what you did to me? To Mina?"

"I don't understand," interrupted Cohen. "Your daughter is really the only thing you care about? She's not the only person in the world."

"She's the only important thing to me," said Kathleen. "Perhaps one day you'll have children of your own, and you'll see. Or"—she eyed Cohen—"perhaps not." She stepped forward suddenly and held a hand to Cohen's temple. Cohen flinched, and for a moment his vision went white. He could see nothing, feel nothing, only a race of emotions and jumbled thoughts. Then Kathleen's hand retreated, and she *tsked*. "You've got protections on you," she said, turning away and continuing to walk. "Set by the Guild. I can't bypass them. I saw enough, though. Poor, lonely little boy, trapped in a body that's all wrong. Do you really think you'll ever be free?"

"That's not how it works," said Cohen. "You don't understand people at all, do you?"

"Don't," Niall cut in. "Don't even talk to her, Cohen."

They stepped out onto the road, and Kathleen crossed her arms, tapping her fingers impatiently. "We're wasting time. Niall, I can track down Jacky the same way I tracked you down, but your little boyfriend will only get in the way. We need to put him somewhere Jacky won't look for him. I'd love to place a spell on him so we'd know if Jacky was attacking him, but unfortunately, I can't, so we need to hide him."

"What, you want me to just hang out in the shrubbery?" snapped Cohen.

"Do you have any friends in town?" Kathleen asked. "Someone Jacky won't know about?"

"I just moved here. I don't really know anyone." Cohen thought. "I guess maybe Myrna might let me stay at her place."

Niall looked confused. "Myrna? The police chief? Are you friends with her?"

"That's good enough for me," sighed Kathleen. "If you didn't know about it, then neither will Jacky." She glanced at Cohen. "Will she let you stay with her?"

"Well...probably, if I explain."

"Do her a favour and don't," said Kathleen. "Let's go. We don't have time for any of this. Jacky could be acquiring the next sacrifice as we speak."

"It's not a matter of trusting you," said Myrna, leading Cohen down the hallway. "It's needing to know whether or not my children are safe. Now, Kelsie is at her boyfriend's for the night, so I don't need to worry about her. This is her bedroom; you can sleep in it, *but*"—she slammed an arm in front of the door just as Cohen was about to enter—"not until you tell me exactly what's going on."

Cohen felt like he was going to cry. "Myrna, I'm *exhausted.*"

"You look exhausted; you look like you've been through hell."

"I have," said Cohen. "But, Myrna, I really *can't* explain."

"I really think you can." Myrna's face was unsympathetic and unimpressed. "Is it something illegal? Are you wanted for smuggling drugs?"

"It's nothing like that, I just—" Cohen sighed. He wanted so badly to go to bed. Maybe Myrna would let him sleep if he told her. Or she'd take him to a padded room and he could sleep there. "It's Niall—"

"Why doesn't that surprise me?"

"He's gotten into something bad. There's an organisation that was doing experiments on him, and they're after him, and there's another escaped prisoner who wants to kill me along with everyone else in the organisation."

"And this isn't a matter to be entrusted to the police because...?"

"Because I think the organisation sort of...owns the police. Or at least has some influence."

"So you don't trust *me*."

"I do, it's just—" Cohen slumped against the wall. "I just want to go to sleep."

Myrna pursed her lips and examined Cohen for a long moment. "Fine—" she began, just as the phone rang. She turned to look at the source of the ringing. "It is the middle of the night; someone had better be—"

Dead.

"Oh no," whispered Cohen.

"What?" Myrna turned back to him.

"Just—" Cohen nodded at the kitchen. "Get the phone."

Myrna gave him another look, then headed to the kitchen. Cohen waited, his stomach doing flip-flops as she picked up. "Hello? Speaking. Kent, is it not something you can—" She went silent for several seconds. "I see. All right,

I'll be right in. You're—you're sure she's all right? Fine, I'll be there." She hung up and swept past Cohen to her bedroom a moment later. "I'm going in to the station," she said shortly, shutting the bedroom door.

"Why?" Cohen could feel his pulse in his fingertips. "What happened?"

There was silence. A minute later, Myrna came out, fully dressed in her uniform, and went into Noleen's room. Cohen hovered at the doorway, listening.

"Mammy's going into work," she told Noleen. "So I'm taking you to Mr and Mrs Blarney's for the night, okay?"

"Okay," Noleen said sleepily, and a moment later Myrna emerged carrying Noleen and a few blankets.

"You can stay here. I don't care now," she said.

"No, Myrna, tell me what's happened!"

"Give me a moment," snapped Myrna, and she headed out the front door. Frustrated, Cohen pulled out his mobile and attempted to call Niall. It went directly to voicemail, which meant that Niall was out of range. He tried again, stepping out onto the front porch, but the result was the same. Myrna returned from the neighbours' shortly after and headed to her police cruiser.

"You have to tell me what's going on. Listen!" shouted Cohen, racing up to her. "Niall might be in danger! What's happened?"

"Another murder," said Myrna shortly, fumbling with her keys. "It—it was Kelsie's boyfriend. She's fine, but...but she saw it happen." She covered her mouth with her hand, leaning against the car for a moment."

"Oh no," said Cohen. "Myrna, did she say who did it? Was—was his heart removed?"

She turned to stare at him. "How did you know that? That's classified information."

Cohen's mind was racing. He had to think, had to figure out what to do. It was imperative that he tell Niall and Kathleen about the murder, so they could try to stop Jacky. Cohen was no longer really in danger, so there was no need for him to hide any longer. If he only had his car, he could go to the stones, try to stop Jacky himself. "Myrna, I need you to bring me somewhere."

"I'm going to the police station to see my daughter," said Myrna. "It can wait."

"It really can't," said Cohen. "I'm sorry. Listen." He really hoped this worked. It had to work. "If I tell you I can bring you to the murderer, that I know where he is and how to stop him, will you do it?"

"You're trying to manipulate me," said Myrna, turning to look at Cohen levelly. "Why don't you just tell me the truth?"

"Because." Cohen gritted his teeth. "You won't believe me."

"Well, you're going to have to try me," said Myrna. "Because I won't be manipulated, and I refuse to work with you unless you tell me exactly what's going on."

"Okay," said Cohen. "Okay, fine and you're going to think I'm crazy, but I guess I have no other choice. This organisation, I guess it's called the Guild. It's a group of people with like, special abilities."

"Special abilities."

"Like, like..." He squinted his eyes shut, remembered exploding beans and magical fire, explosions of light and killer trees. Myrna was not going to believe this. "Like psychic abilities."

"All right," said Myrna.

"I know it seems crazy," said Cohen. "But I've seen it. Niall showed me. He calls himself a witch and he can do...things."

Myrna raised her eyebrows. "All right."

"You don't believe me," sighed Cohen. "You think I'm crazy, don't you?"

Myrna just shook her head. "Not really. I'm a police officer, Cohen. I've seen plenty of crazy things."

"So you do believe me."

Myrna crossed her arms in front of her and stared at him, her lips pursed. Finally, she shook her head. "I don't know what to believe, but for some godforsaken reason, I trust you. So you'd better be telling the truth."

"I am," said Cohen weakly.

"Right," said Myrna. "Where do you need to go, then?"

Cohen tried to call Niall again as they drove, hoping and praying that he would answer. He kept remembering what Niall had said about how every powerful magic-user was required to sign themselves over to the Guild in blood. If Jacky summoned the Titan and told it to destroy the Guild, how many people would die? Would Niall be one of them? Would Cohen too? Niall and Kathleen had both said the Guild had placed protections on him, so maybe that meant he belonged to them too. He didn't want to die.

"No more reception," said Cohen hollowly as they drove over a hilltop. Myrna glanced at her phone as well.

"I have a radio," she said. "I can call for backup."

"You can't," said Cohen shortly. "It would be dangerous for them, and anyway, they might belong to the Guild."

"So turn this Jacky into them," said Myrna. "If he's that dangerous."

Cohen felt sick to his stomach. "Niall said Jacky would rather die."

"Then those are his choices," replied Myrna shortly. "He can be turned in to the authorities, or he can die." She paused. "That's why you asked me that before at dinner, isn't it? It wasn't for your book."

"No." Cohen felt himself shrinking into the seat.

They drove in silence for a while, until Cohen recognised the turn-off he'd driven down earlier that night (it seemed so long ago now) and directed Myrna down it. Soon his car came into sight. Myrna pulled up next to it, and they both got out.

"You can go back to the station now," said Cohen. "Kelsie probably needs you."

Myrna shook her head, and Cohen realised that she was pulling her gun from her belt. "I think I'm needed right here."

Cohen didn't know what to do. He hadn't intended to put Myrna in danger, but at the same time he felt safer with her here.

"Who are we looking for?" Myrna asked him. "Niall?"

"Yes." Cohen swallowed. "Or Kathleen. She's with the Guild, but she's agreed to help Niall stop Jacky."

"And what is it we need to tell them?"

"That Jacky's killed again and taken another heart. After this, he only needs Kathleen's. We need to warn her and stop Jacky if we can." Where to look though? Cohen stared up the hill, where he knew the stones were. Jacky could be there already. He could have already found and killed Kathleen, or be about to. They couldn't just leave. "Come on," he told Myrna. "This way."

The grass was drier now, the sky darker, although the stars blazed even brighter. There were no flashes in the sky this time, but he remembered the way. It had only been a few hours since he'd been here last. His heart was racing at the memory. He'd narrowly escaped being killed last time, but here he was again.

"I hope Niall and Kathleen are here," he whispered. "If it's just Jacky, we're probably in for it."

"Lucky you've got me with you," said Myrna, and Cohen nodded. He didn't like putting Myrna in danger, but he knew she couldn't just stand by any more than he could.

"What is this?" said Myrna, nearly tripping over the line of magical stones and sticks as they crossed it. As soon as they did so, Cohen felt something. A familiar prickling on the back of his neck, colder and darker than he'd felt before. He whipped his head around to the source of the feeling. It was coming from over the hill, where the stones were. Jacky was doing magic of some sort. Was he sacrificing the lover's heart? Or the witch's?

"Can you feel that?" he asked Myrna.

"I don't know," said Myrna, but she was looking around, towards the stones as well, and Cohen thought she could.

"We couldn't feel it outside the circle because it blocks magic," Cohen muttered. "Oh!"

"What?" said Myrna as Cohen frantically began to kick at the rocks and stones, breaking the line wherever he could. "What are you doing?"

"I'm breaking it," explained Cohen. "That way, if Niall and Kathleen aren't here already, they'll feel it and come, and so will the rest of the Guild, probably. Not quite as good as a phone, but it'll have to do." *Please, please let it work.* Cohen's heart dropped as he realised that if the Guild captured Jacky, they would probably get Niall back too. He couldn't let that happen. They had to stop Jacky before the Guild could get at either of them. "Come on, we've got to go."

"I hope you know what you're doing," whispered Myrna furiously, but she followed him up the hill. He peered over, seeing nothing but the standing stones, peaceful against the night sky. But his instincts were telling him a different story.

"There's definitely something going on down there," he whispered. "Can't you feel it?"

Myrna was staring at the stones, her face taut but her eyes wide. "You're right," she whispered. "Like a chill."

Cohen's heart was beating sporadically again. What if it was too late? What if Niall was down there right now? What could he possibly do?

"I have to go," he whispered, starting down the hill.

"We should wait for your friends!" Myrna whispered after him.

"They might already be down there!" Cohen hissed back. "We have to stop him."

"You're going to get yourself killed, lad."

"I'm trying not to. If I don't go, a lot of people could die."

"All right," said Myrna, and she grabbed Cohen's arm as he started down the hill. "But you should let me go. I don't like risking civilians."

Cohen swallowed. "I'm not exactly just a civilian. For one thing, I'm protected, and anyway, if we don't stop him, I might be one of the ones who die. I have to do this."

Myrna shook her head as if she had stopped trying to keep up with Cohen's explanations. "Fine. Let's go."

They reached the stones, stepping in amongst the tall, dark shadows. The feeling was stronger now, emanating from somewhere below him. It made him want to be sick, to curl up and hide. "There must be an entrance underground," he said. "Look for one."

"I've been here before," said Myrna, looking around anyway. "There's never been—oh. Here."

Cohen came around the stone she was gesturing at and saw that one of the stones had fallen sideways to reveal a set of stone stairs heading down. It had obviously been done recently. The upturned earth was still fresh. Cohen peered in and thought he could see a stairway leading down.

"I'm going," he whispered. "You should stay here."

"I think you should let me go first," replied Myrna.

Cohen shook his head. "It's safer for me. Jacky will probably just kill you, but he knows I'm valuable to Niall. He might keep me alive so he can use me to control him. It sounds terrible but…"

"Is there a danger Niall might try to save you?" asked Myrna. "Instead of doing what needs to be done?"

Cohen swallowed. "Yes," he whispered, his voice cracking. "But he'll be with Kathleen, and I know she won't hesitate. All right, I'm going down." He took a few gulps of air and slowly lowered himself down onto the narrow staircase. A wet chill crept up from the earth, and he looked up at Myrna, trying not to panic. "If Niall and Kathleen show up, tell them what's going on."

"If I hear anything, I'm coming down after you," Myrna replied. "I hope you know what you're doing. You're certainly brave enough; I'll give you that."

Cohen didn't know if he was brave or just stupid. He certainly didn't feel brave. As the light from above receded and he was enveloped in cold darkness, he felt more and more like he was on the verge of panicking. Just when he was about to give up and go back, he saw a light ahead. It wasn't a lot, only a bit of moonlight, but when he reached the ground and turned the corner, he could see clearly.

In the centre of a vast chamber carved from cold stone were statues taller than any human, with blank stone eyes. The smell of dust and earth was nearly suffocating. He shouldn't be here. No one should be here. There was an altar of some sort at the base, and a man kneeling in front of it, breathing heavily.

A gasp caught in Cohen's throat, and he whipped his head back around the corner. Whatever Jacky had been doing, he seemed to be finished; the cold feeling was gone, leaving only emptiness and the echoing noises of Jacky's breathing. He didn't see Niall or Kathleen anywhere. Hopefully, that meant they were still safe, and Jacky hadn't done the last sacrifice yet. Either that or he had left their bodies somewhere. Cohen's stomach lurched at the thought. Either way, he should get out of here.

"Hello." Jacky was in front of him suddenly, grinning wickedly, his hand around Cohen's neck. "Fancy seeing you here."

Cohen tried to scream, but it was cut off as Jacky's hand tightened. He couldn't breathe, and Jacky's fingers were pressing into the bruises left from the branches earlier. His vision spotted and went white as Jacky dragged him towards the altar.

"I'd hoped I could use your heart, but you know how it is. Sometimes you have to make sacrifices." He laughed and slammed Cohen against the altar. His neck free but the wind knocked out of him, Cohen tried desperately to breathe. He could smell blood and something rotten. "You'll be the perfect bait."

Cohen choked and drew in a wheezing breath, desperately tried to get his brain working again. Bait. So that meant he was waiting for Niall and Kathleen. They were alive. Niall was alive. But Jacky could kill Cohen right now. He had no reason not to. Cohen hadn't realised until this moment, breathing raggedly and shaking on the dirt floor, how badly he didn't want to die. He'd only just begun his transition. He didn't want to be remembered by his old name. Last night at this time, he'd been sleeping next to Niall. There was so much he wanted, but looking back, he knew he'd make all the same decisions again.

Niall. He tried to think of Niall. He'd be coming soon. Jacky didn't know that Cohen had broken the wards. They, or the Guild—someone would come. He hoped whoever it was would get here soon, before Jacky had time to set up a trap, and before Jacky hurt him and Myrna too badly. He'd been hurt so much tonight. He didn't think he could live through too much more.

He choked back a sob. *Stall.* He had to stall Jacky. "They don't know where I am." He managed to cough. "They think I'm safe at home."

"Really?" Jacky touched a hand to Cohen's temple, and there was a sharp, painful flash. He brought his hand away, hissing, and Cohen felt a light tickle as the amulet around his neck turned to ash. "Goddamn witch and her stupid tricks," Jacky spat. "I'll kill her. Well, it doesn't matter if you're lying. They'll figure out where you are anyway, eventually. They'll come, and I'll be ready for them. I think I'll wait to kill you until he's watching. So he can see the light leave your eyes."

Cohen's head snapped back as the string broke, and he struggled to focus his eyes. Something moved behind Jacky. A light.

"Jacky!" said a woman's voice, and then Jacky was thrown off his feet and backwards into one of the statues, narrowly missing the altar. It crumbled under the force, the stones hitting the floor heavily, and Cohen flinched. Jacky hissed and sat up from among the rubble, and Cohen caught sight of Kathleen's blonde hair as she rushed towards Jacky. There was a loud ripping noise, and a large piece of the ground in front of him lifted of its own accord and flew towards Jacky. Cohen turned his head just in time to see him throw his arms up, shattering the packed earth into pieces.

Cohen had thought Jacky and Niall had been fighting before, but he saw now that had only been a dance. Jacky and Kathleen were fighting tooth and nail, like a clash between gods. Jacky was furiously blasting magic at

Kathleen, destroying the walls and the ground around them. But Kathleen was controlling that ground, ripping and shredding it and moulding it into a fierce onslaught of rocks and earth.

Cohen jerked as a hand grabbed his arm, and he turned into Niall's embrace. "Are you all right?" Niall gasped, and Cohen shoved him away.

"Don't worry about me. You have to help Kathleen!"

"No, we've got to get you out of here!" Niall insisted.

"Niall, no! Stop Jacky!"

Niall gave a strangled gasp as Jacky appeared next to him and clamped a hand to the back of his neck. He screamed and tried to pull away, but Jacky had a vice-like grip on him, and Cohen could see it burning Niall's neck. Cohen lunged forward to try and stop him, but it was too late. Jacky had wrapped a leg around Niall and an arm, and the other was held between their heads and glowing like a miniature sun. "Stop!" he shouted gleefully at Kathleen. "Stop, or I'll kill us both."

Kathleen froze. Cohen tried to dart towards them again, but Jacky turned and held him at bay as well. What could he do? Would Jacky really kill Niall? Could he risk it? Somewhere in the back of his mind, Cohen knew he must, but he couldn't make himself move.

"Jacky!" screamed Niall, his voice thick with panic.

"I'll do it, Niall," laughed Jacky. "Don't either of you doubt that I'll do it."

"Kathleen!" shouted Niall. "Stop him!"

"She won't," said Jacky quietly to Niall. "She won't stop me because if both of us are dead, then she's failed, and it's lights out for little—" He turned to look at Kathleen. "What's her name? Mina?"

"Don't say her name," hissed Kathleen.

"Right," said Jacky. "Well, Niall, walk this way." He took a step towards Kathleen, and then another. Kathleen stood still, her face twisted in rage. Finally they were close enough to touch. Jacky extinguished the light from his hands and pressed both hands to Niall, shoving him to the side. Cohen lunged forward to catch him as he fell, so he heard the noise before he saw what Jacky had done.

A thick squelching noise, and a crack, and then a wheeze from Kathleen. Cohen turned and screamed, his hand flying to his mouth. Jacky had thrust his hand into Kathleen's chest. Slowly, they sank to the ground, Jacky laughing as he dug deep. Kathleen's body spasmed, and blood spurted from her mouth.

"You failed," Jacky whispered to Kathleen as his hand moved around in her chest, snapping the arteries and sending blood spurting. "You know that? Your daughter, what's her name? Mina." He pronounced her name slowly with venom and delight. "I'm going to find her, and when I do, I'm going to kill her. I am going to *tear her apart.*"

A deafening bang echoed around the cavern. Cohen's head snapped towards the entrance of the cavern, and he drew a sharp breath.

Myrna stood there, her feet spread and her hands holding her gun steady in front of her.

Jacky gave a wheeze and then a cough. Cohen turned to look at him and heard Niall gasp. Jacky looked confused. He pulled his hand from Kathleen's chest with a thick, sucking noise and touched it to his chest. It was hard to tell where Kathleen's blood ended and his began, at first, until it started to seep out into the fabric of his hoodie. He gasped and gave a wild, feral scream that cut off prematurely; then he fell sideways with a thump that echoed through the room. Cohen instantly knew he was dead. He could see his eyes, glazed and distant. It was like looking into eternity.

"Jacky," whispered Niall, and Cohen grabbed him and held him tight. Niall was shaking all over. Myrna was there a moment later, grabbing and shaking Cohen by the shoulder, and he looked up at her. He felt as if his reflexes were slow, and everything was a little too bright.

"Tell me I've just shot the right person, Cohen," she said.

Cohen nodded wordlessly. He felt Niall stir and get up, rushing over to the bodies. There was blood pooling on the dirt floor, but he knelt in it, regardless.

"Niall," said Cohen tentatively, and Niall let out a sob.

"I know I'm awake now," he said. "This can't possibly be a dream." He looked at Cohen, his eyes red but focused. "They're coming now."

"I know," said Cohen. He felt a sob creeping up his throat, but he couldn't even piece together why. Not when there was so much crowding his consciousness. "You have to go."

"I have to destroy all of this," said Niall. "I have to; the Guild can't know what happened here. And you two— you both need to go right now."

"Niall, I don't want to lose you—"

"I know!" shouted Niall. "So you have to go right now. You both have to go, and you have to pretend that none of this ever happened, and you were never involved with me. Cohen, listen." He touched his hands to Cohen's cheeks and pressed their foreheads together. "Remember what you said? About us running away together?"

Cohen nodded; the misty fantasy of him and Niall together, far away and safe, sprung up again, fragile and hazy.

"It can only work if the Guild has no idea that you ever knew me, and no reason to think that you did."

"But..." Cohen's heart was racing again. He was thinking about how the Guild had tracked Niall and Jacky down, what they'd done to them, how they had used Kathleen's daughter against her. How they were part of the government. Part of everything. "Niall, that will never work. They'll know I'm connected to you. I bailed you out of jail. I came here with Myrna to help you. They'll see her memories. They'll see *my* memories. They've got me under surveillance, right? Under their control?"

"They have," said Niall. "But—"

"Then I don't have a choice," said Cohen. Tears were welling up in his eyes. This was never going to be all right. Nothing was. "Don't you see, Niall? They'll use me to get to you. At the very least they'll watch me forever to see if I ever contact you. And they might do worse. They might use me as bait. And Myrna, and Myrna's daughters." He glanced at Myrna, who was staring at him stonily. "And if I go with you, try to escape, they'll use my family. There's *nothing* we can do."

Niall took a few steps back from Cohen. "You're right," he said. "Of course, you're right. There's only one thing to do, isn't there?" He glanced down at Kathleen and Jacky's bodies. "I have to turn myself in."

"What?" Cohen gasped, realising at once that he was right, while every fibre of his being rejected it. "You can't."

"Of course I can!" shouted Niall. "I was willing to sacrifice everything to stop people from dying, wasn't I? Well, this is the result!" He stared at Cohen, and Cohen could see the fear in his eyes. "No," said Niall after a moment. "No, I've got a better idea." He looked at Myrna.

"What?" said Cohen. "What are you doing?"

"I don't want to go back there," said Niall levelly to Myrna. "I'd rather die. They'll use me to do things I don't want to do. They'll make me into something I'm not. Myrna, Jacky would rather have died. And so would I."

Myrna stared at him for a long moment. Then she unhitched her gun from her belt.

"No!" said Cohen. "Myrna, no, you can't!"

"I can." Myrna's face was still, her eyes dark. "I would do anything if it means protecting my daughters, Cohen."

"No." Cohen shook his head. "No, that's just like Kathleen. They're making you all like her."

"She's choosing to sacrifice one person for the lives of many," said Niall. His voice was shaking, his face devoid of colour. Cohen could see his lips trembling. More than anything he wanted to kiss them and make everything okay. "She's nothing like Kathleen."

"Well I'm not letting this happen," said Cohen. He glanced around, to the altar with the withered hearts, the bodies of Jacky and Kathleen on the floor. Kathleen's body was losing blood fast, the cavity of her chest ripped open, with her organs on full display. She didn't look real anymore. And that was a good thing.

Cohen took a deep breath. Niall was looking at him, and he couldn't see that dead, hopeless look in his eyes, not for a moment more. He lunged at Kathleen's body and shoved his hand into her chest, tugging on the heart. Luckily, Jacky had all but detached it already.

"Cohen!" Niall screamed and ran at him, but it was too late. Cohen had tugged the heart free and turned to the altar, slamming it down into the last alcove, next to the others. The room went dim. Cohen gasped as he felt the air sucked from his lungs. He drew a breath, but instead of air, something else flowed into him, like pure darkness. Then the pain began.

To say it was like nothing he had ever felt before would be an understatement. It was more than just pain. Sickness and darkness. Hatred that seemed not completely his own. His dysphoria rose to the surface, threatening to choke him, like a live beast burrowing into his soul. His body felt small and fragile and not enough to contain what was within him now.

Who has chained me?

The voice echoed in his head. The pain was so great that he couldn't feel or hear anything, but it didn't matter. This was inside him, so much inside him that he felt his body might break at any moment.

It wasn't me. I didn't chain you. I've released you. But...but you have to do what I say.

So it would seem I am chained, replied the voice, and Cohen realised that was probably the case. As long as he held on, the darkness was contained in his body. But it hurt so much.

I don't want anyone to die. It was hard to think, but that was his most prevalent thought. *I-I don't want anyone to die or get hurt.*

Then we are very different, you and I.

Cohen tried to blink, tried to move his limbs, but nothing worked. His body was exerting all its energy to keep the vast force inside of him. He thought it might kill him. Where was he? Where were Niall and Myrna right now? Were they touching him? Trying to stop him?

What is it you desire, creature of mud?

What did he desire? He desired Niall, and safety, and to not have a body that fought him at all angles. But those were just little things. Things he could live without. There was more at stake. *Do you know about the Guild?*

I saw the dark mind of the one who came before you. Yes, I know of the Guild. He wanted them dead.

I don't want them dead, said Cohen. *I just want them to leave everyone alone.*

They will die before they do that.

I don't want anyone to die.

Then you were unwise to release me.

Niall had said that summoning the demon was the stupidest thing he'd ever done. Cohen realised this just topped that. *I haven't released you yet.*

Cohen felt the Titan bristle inside. **If you release me, I shall see that whatever you desire comes to fruition, little creature of mud.**

Think, think, think. This was what Cohen was good at. He may be short and round and clumsy and trapped, but at least he was smart. He needed to use his brain right now. *If I release you, you need to promise never to hurt anyone, or—* He thought long and hard. He had to get this right. *—or do anything that will cause someone pain. Ever.*

The creature's essence boiled and rumbled inside of Cohen. It didn't like that. **Very well.**

And, you have to release the Guild's hold on Niall. Make it so they've never even heard of him. So even if they were to come face to face with him, they won't care about him, or anyone he is involved with. Can you do that?

I can. But— The darkness seemed to laugh. **Your lover has powerful magic, does he not? Do you wish for him to go unchecked? Why not just release me?**

He's not going to misuse it. But the Titan had a point. The Guild had good intentions, too, but too much power had corrupted them as well. *But he doesn't want it anyway. You can take it away.*

You are very stupid and brave, little creature of mud. Your mind is full of light. There is too much of you for your body.

I like my body, thought Cohen firmly. He didn't know what the Titan was insinuating, but it sounded a little transphobic to him. *I'll keep it, thanks.*

You are going to die soon. Your body will return to the mud, your soul to the magic. Would you not rather live forever?

We're not having this conversation. Although the pain his body was in right now was tempting him. Was he going to die right now? Would he ever be able to come back from what he'd just done? *I gave you my terms.*

And I accept them.

Cohen felt like his body was breaking apart. Darkness flowed out of him, through every opening in his body and out his pores. Suddenly, his body felt very heavy and dysphoric. Was this all he had? Was this all his body would ever be? Little and broken and not enough. Every nerve ending was in pain; every part of his stupid little wrong human body was obvious to him. He sobbed, pulling his arms to his chest, and fell forward. Why had he refused death? This was torture.

"Cohen!" Niall's voice echoed in his head and then shouted too loudly next to his ear. "Cohen! Are you all right?"

"I'm fine," he murmured. "I'm fine, Niall; just don't—don't touch me." He felt wrong. Every part of him felt wrong. He shuddered, over and over again. He felt nauseous and oh so tired.

"Where's the Titan?" asked Niall. "Cohen, what happened?"

"It's gone," said Cohen. "It flew away. I told it... I told it not to hurt anyone."

"What else did you tell it?" Cohen could tell that Niall wanted to touch him. He wished he could.

"I told it to take away your magic," he murmured. He felt dizzy. Which way was up? He thought he was falling sideways onto the ground. He was going to puke. "I told it to make the Guild forget about you." He did puke then, turning onto his side and heaving his guts out. Myrna grabbed him and helped him turn. She seemed to know the exact way to hold him so he didn't choke.

"That was so *stupid*," said Niall. "Cohen, you could have died!"

"So could you," said Cohen. "I think I need to go to the hospital." With that, he felt his head spinning, and darkness claimed him again. But it was an empty kind this time, like the darkness and relief of sleep, and he fell into it willingly.

Epilogue

He awoke in a hospital. He knew it was a hospital immediately because the ceiling was tiled, and he smelled chemicals and sanitiser. For a moment he just lay, staring at the ceiling and wondering if he'd imagined the whole thing. Then he heard Niall's voice and knew he hadn't.

"You're awake!"

"Yeah," murmured Cohen. "Of course I'm awake; sleeping is boring."

Niall leaned over him. His eyes were bloodshot, his hair a mess, and his face unshaven. "I should call the doctors."

"You look terrible," murmured Cohen. He was dimly becoming aware of things like the scratchy hospital blanket and the fact that he wasn't wearing his binder. "Shouldn't you be hiding?"

"I don't need to," said Niall. "The Guild already interviewed me and Myrna and let us go. They don't seem to know or care who I am."

Cohen smiled blearily. "Good. How long have I been asleep? Also, where are we?"

"Three days. Hospital in Dublin. Your family's here."

"Oh, great. I don't want to see them."

Niall looked confused. "Why not?"

"I just—" Cohen blinked, suddenly aware that he had a massive headache. His eyes teared up in reaction to it. "How will I explain everything to them?"

"You don't need to explain anything to them. You were kidnapped by a murderer, but Myrna took care of him. I'm your boyfriend, which is why I came with you to Dublin."

"You're my boyfriend?" Cohen grinned. He still felt incredibly dopey. "What do my parents think of that?"

"They, um, think it means you'd like to go back to being a girl."

Cohen sighed heavily. "See, I don't want to talk to them."

"Cohen!" Halley's voice ripped right through Cohen's headache. She was next to him in a moment, although blurry in his peripheral vision. "You're awake! I'll get Mam and Dad."

"Okay, fine," said Cohen, accepting his fate. "Halley."

Halley turned back to him as she was leaving the room. "It's good to see you," said Cohen. Halley took a moment to smile at him and then rushed off.

"I want to get out of here as soon as possible," Cohen told Niall.

"Where do you want to go?" asked Niall. "I mean, I thought I might visit my family in Cork."

"Your family," said Cohen, jumping up.

"Yeah," said Niall. "But it might be better to wait, make sure the Titan's effects are permanent."

"Oh." Cohen stared at Niall, trying to will his fuzzy brain to remember. "Your magic. Is it...?"

"Gone," said Niall. "I can still do witchcraft, but that's it. Thank you, by the way. I—" He heaved a sigh. "I never wanted it."

"I know." Cohen was silent for a moment, before remembering. "And Jacky and Kathleen?"

Niall swallowed. "The, um...the Guild recovered their bodies. Myrna says she went back to the site, but it was closed off."

Cohen's parents arrived a moment later, and his conversation with Niall was cut off. They stayed and chatted for several hours, until at last Cohen managed to convince them to go home for the night. Niall sneaked back in just before visiting hours ended and planted a kiss on Cohen's forehead.

"You saved my life," he told Cohen quietly. "You saved...everything."

"I didn't," said Cohen sadly. The time with his family had given him a chance to come down from his high of having survived and realise how far short of perfect everything was. "The Guild is still out there. They're doing horrible things. What are we supposed to do?"

"I don't know if there's anything we can do," said Niall.

"Fuck that," said Cohen. "There's got to be something."

"You have time," said Niall. "We've got time to figure everything out. You can't change everything, Cohen."

"Maybe not." Cohen shook his head. "But I can damn well try."

Niall had to leave then. He kissed Cohen's forehead again, and then his lips, a lingering kiss full of promise, and then he left.

Cohen lay in the darkness, unable to sleep for a long while, but with nothing else to do. He wanted to get up and wander around, but his body felt like lead, and he was connected to an IV. He looked around for a book, but saw nothing. The people in the beds next to him were asleep, so he couldn't watch TV. He sat, resigning himself to boredom.

There was a shadow at the foot of his bed, on the green textured linoleum of the floor, and he stared at it for several minutes, trying to figure out what was making it. The only light in the room was the warm glow from the hallway and the moonlight through the window, but there was nothing in either of those directions to make that shadow.

As Cohen continued staring at it, his eyes grew tired, and his vision wavered, making him think for a minute the shadow was moving. It swirled and began to creep along the floor, to the night table next to Cohen. Then it latched onto the IV stand and pulled itself up next to Cohen. It wavered and shimmered, and then a body and a head formed. Dark, shadow-black eyes blinked slowly.

Hello again, little creature of mud.

About J.K. Pendragon

J.K. Pendragon is a Canadian author with a love of all things romantic and fantastical. They first came to the queer fiction community through m/m romance, but soon began to branch off into writing all kinds of queer fiction. As a bisexual and genderqueer person, J.K. is dedicated to producing diverse, entertaining fiction that showcases characters across the rainbow spectrum, and provides queer characters with the happy endings they are so often denied.

J.K. currently resides in British Columbia, Canada with a boyfriend, a cat, and a large collection of artisanal teas that they really need to get around to drinking. They are always happy to chat and can be reached at:

Email
jes.k.pendragon@gmail.com

Twitter
@JKPendragon

Instagram
jesthependragon

Website
jkpendragon.com

Other NineStar books by this author

Witch, Cat, and Cobb

Junior Hero Blues

Sea Lover

Also from NineStar Press

Dinner at the Blue Moon Café by Rick R. Reed

A monster moves through the darkest night, lit only by the full moon, taking them, one by one, from Seattle's gay gathering areas.

In an atmosphere of spine-tingling fear, Thad Matthews finds his first true love cooking in an Italian restaurant called The Blue Moon Cafe. Sam Lupino is everything Thad has ever hoped for in a man: virile, sexy as hell, kind, and...he can cook!

As the pair's love heats up, so do the questions. Who is the killer preying on Seattle's gay men? What secrets is Sam's Sicilian family hiding? And, more important, why do Sam's unexplained disappearances always coincide with the full moon?

When the secrets are finally revealed, is Thad and Sam's love for one another strong enough to weather the horrific revelations revealed by the light of the full moon?

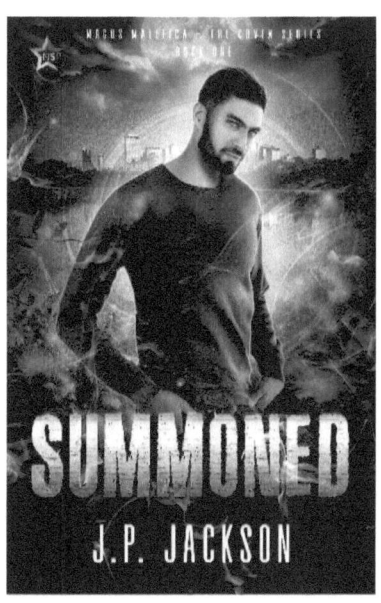

Summoned by J.P. Jackson

Devid Khandelwal desperately wants to experience the supernatural. After years of studying everything from crystals to tarot to spellcasting, nothing has happened that would tell him the Shadow Realm is real. And that kills Dev. As a last-ditch resort, he purchases a summoning board, an occult tool that will grant him his ultimate desires.

Cameron Habersham is Dev's best friend. Cam loves Dev like a brother and will do anything for him, as long as he looks good doing it. So when Dev asks him to perform the summoning board's ritual, he reluctantly agrees, but he knows nothing will come of it. Nothing ever does.

However, within a day, Dev and Cam's lives are turned upside down as wishes begin to come true. They discover the existence of a supernatural world beyond their imagination, but peace between the species is tenuous at best.

Dev finally gets to see the Shadow Realm, meets the man of his dreams, and is inducted into the local male coven. But for all the desires that were summoned into existence, Dev soon realizes the magical community dances the line between good and evil, and Cam ends up on the wrong side of everything.

The old adage is true: Be careful what you wish for.

Elemental Ride by Mel Eight

Rawley isn't the type to crush hard and fast on anyone, but he's helpless when it comes to Reign, the new mail carrier. Even his bikes and his job as enforcer for a local motorcycle gang, the center of his world, don't compare to his interest in Reign. Unfortunately, Reign doesn't seem to be as interested—but secrets and magic have a way of turning everything upside down and Rawley discovers he not only loves one man, he loves four.

Connect with NineStar Press

www.ninestarpress.com

www.facebook.com/ninestarpress

www.facebook.com/groups/NineStarNiche

www.twitter.com/ninestarpress

www.instagram.com/ninestarpress